NONE THE WISER

A DETECTIVE MARK TURPIN NOVEL

RACHEL AMPHLETT

ALSO BY RACHEL AMPHLETT

The Detective Kay Hunter series

Scared to Death

Will to Live

One to Watch

Hell to Pay

Call to Arms

Gone to Ground

Bridge to Burn

Cradle to Grave

Turn to Dust

The English Spy mysteries

Assassins Hunted

Assassins Vengeance

Assassins Retribution

The Dan Taylor spy novels

White Gold

Under Fire

Three Lives Down

Behind the Wire

Standalone titles

Look Closer

The Friend Who Lied

Mistake Creek

Before Nightfall

Connect with Rachel Amphlett

www.rachelamphlett.com

CHAPTER ONE

Seamus Carter dropped to his knees.

His voice was little more than a murmur, rising and falling with the rhythm of the prayer.

Exhaustion threatened, and he tried to take strength from the subtext, a momentary sense of calm easing the guilt that had gnawed away at him for days. He kept his eyes closed in meditation a while longer, savouring the tentative peace that enveloped him.

No-one would disturb him.

He was alone – the pub that stood on the other side of the boundary wall with his church had a live band playing tonight. He had heard the thumping bass line as he had been praying, and none of his parishioners were likely to visit at this time of night.

Easing himself from a kneeling position, he genuflected as he gazed up at the wooden crucifix above the altar, and then bowed his head in a final, silent prayer.

Seamus blinked, his trance-like state leaving him as soon as he moved away from the altar.

Despite his efforts, the self-loathing remained, and he scowled.

It wasn't meant to be like this.

He stomped along the aisle towards the vestry, reached into his pocket for a bubble pack of antacids, then popped and swallowed two.

His thoughts turned to the Sunday morning service, and the uplifting sermon he was struggling to write.

The events of the previous week had shaken him, and he needed to excuse his fear.

Addressing the congregation would be a tincture, a way to soothe the wound that had been opened.

Crossing the remaining length of the nave, he pushed through the door to his office and sank into the hard wooden chair at his desk. It faced the wall, a plain wooden cross above his head.

The room had no windows, which he preferred. The setting enabled him to meditate upon his words as he crafted carefully phrased sentences to spread the word of his God.

He tapped the trackpad on the laptop, and, as the screen blinked to life, he manoeuvred the cursor over the music app, selected a compilation of violin sonatas, and closed his eyes as the music washed over him.

He smiled.

Two years ago, the church cleaner had entered the room and emitted a sharp, shocked gasp at the loud trance music emanating from the computer. After he'd calmed her and tried to convince her that, often, his best sermons were written at one hundred and twenty beats per minute, she'd continued with her dusting, although she'd eyed him warily. He'd resisted the urge to educate her musical tastes further with the progressive rock of 1970s Pink Floyd.

Seamus read through the words he had typed an hour ago, and frowned. He deleted the last sentence, cracked his knuckles and then stabbed two fingers at the keyboard in an attempt to convey the thoughts that troubled him.

Perhaps in sharing his own foibles, he would find retribution.

The stack of paperwork at his elbow fluttered as a cold breeze slapped against the back of his neck, and he rubbed the skin, his eyes never leaving the screen.

He would check all the doors and windows before leaving tonight, but now he had found his flow, the sermon was almost complete.

A shuffling noise reached his ears before he

became aware of someone standing behind him, a moment before a rope snaked around his neck.

Seamus lashed out in fear, shoving the chair backwards. Terror gripped him as the noose grew taut.

A gloved hand slapped his right ear, sending shards of pain into his skull, and he cried out in pain as his assailant moved into view.

Black mask, black sweatshirt, black jeans.

'There's money in the box in the filing cabinet over there. My wallet is in my trouser pocket.'

Before he could recover from the shock, his right wrist was fastened to the arm of the chair with a plastic tie.

His left fist flailed, then Seamus cried out as he was punched in the balls, all the air rushing from his lungs in one anguished gasp.

He panted as his left wrist was secured to the chair, and tried to focus his thoughts.

'What do you want?'

The words dried on his lips as he heard the warble in his rasping voice, the unsteadiness that betrayed the lie.

Eyes glared at him from slits within a black hood, but no words came.

Instead, the figure moved behind him.

Bile rose in his throat as the rope tightened under his Adam's apple.

'Help!'

His cry was instinctive, desperate – and useless.

Restricted by the rope around his neck, his voice was little more than a croak, broken and shattered.

He twisted in his seat, nostrils flaring as he tugged at the ties that bound his wrists to the arms of the chair.

He couldn't move.

He gagged, struggling to swallow.

Without warning, the rope jerked, forcing his chin towards the ceiling and burning his throat.

A single tear rolled over his cheek as a wetness formed between his legs, heat rising to his face while his attacker crouched at the back of the chair, securing the rope.

He had known it would come to this, one day.

The figure said nothing, and edged around his body, peering into his eyes before raising a knife to Seamus's face.

A gloved hand gripped his jaw, forcing his mouth open as the priest panted for air.

The blade traced around each eye socket, millimetres away from his face.

I don't want to die.

His eyes bulged as the knife moved to his cheek, his plea little more than a whimper.

Seamus gagged at the rope cutting into his neck, fighting against the pressure in his lungs.

I can't breathe.

A searing pain tore into his tongue, slicing through sinew and tendons before the knife flashed in front of his eyes, blood dripping from the blade, and, as Seamus's body convulsed, the figure before him began to speak.

'Forgive me, Father, for I have sinned...'

CHAPTER TWO

Jan West aimed the key fob at the car, and only relaxed once she saw the indicator lights flash.

The area had developed a reputation for petty theft, and given the car wasn't hers to start with, she wasn't prepared to take any risks. Nor was she prepared to pay the extortionate parking fees demanded by the local council for what would be a short stay.

She turned away from the vehicle, slipped her keys into her leather handbag and buttoned her woollen coat while making her way across the cracked surface of the car park.

Pushing through a gap next to the barred metal gate, she swore under her breath as she slipped in mud-flecked gravel that had congealed next to the verge due to the number of dog walkers who used the route on a regular basis and had churned up the rudimentary path.

She regained her balance, throwing her arms out to her sides, and hoped to hell no-one she knew had seen her. She glanced over her shoulder but the car park remained deserted, save for her vehicle. Peering at the mud clinging to her month-old black suede shoes, she groaned and tried to wipe off the worst on the long grass beside the path. Her eyes fell to her wrist, her watch catching the weak sunlight.

'Crap.'

She could have saved time and cut across the middle of the meadow to the river that twisted and turned its way through the market town, but one look at the boggy earth and she decided she'd take the long way around.

The narrow gravel path soon disappeared, making way for a grassy route worn away by walkers, the stench of rotten vegetation pungent on the damp morning air.

She stood to one side as she spotted a pair of brightly clothed men jog towards her, eyeing them warily as they drew closer and removing her hands from her pockets.

Their heavy breathing sent faint clouds of vapour into the air, and one of them nodded to her as he passed before he set his focus back to his route, several steps ahead of his companion.

The two figures receded into the distance, and Jan noted that instead of going through the gate to the car park, they continued towards an archway under the stone bridge that spanned the river further downstream.

To her left, the backs of a row of cottages flanked the meadow, the landscape a bleak contrast to the busy main road the buildings faced.

She peered over the low wall into the different gardens, taking in the rubbish bins, children's toys discarded haphazardly, and brightly coloured laundry hanging out to dry on washing lines.

Raising her gaze to the clouds tumbling overhead, she thought it a little optimistic of the residents to expect anything to dry that day.

The noise of traffic reached her ears, the narrow bridge over the river adding to the morning congestion problems, despite having been widened three times over the centuries. The market town simply wasn't designed for the number of cars, trucks, and people that descended on it every day.

When she reached the end of the row of cottages, she turned right and began to follow the towpath, with the river to her left.

The waters had receded considerably since the

early spring floods, although a pervading stench of damp assaulted her senses as the earth continued to dry out. She eyed a swan as it floated past. It glared at her disdainfully before paddling off towards its mate that bobbed about on the water near the opposite bank.

Breathing a sigh of relief, she turned her attention to the row of boats further up the towpath.

Modern cruisers dipped and rose on the water alongside brightly painted narrowboats, the creak of ropes on moorings breaking the silence. As she passed the boats, she kept her senses alert while her eyes roamed over the different shapes and sizes.

She glanced over her shoulder, but no-one followed.

She slowed and pulled out a scrap of paper from her pocket, and then lifted her gaze and squinted towards the boats, realising the one she sought was at the far end of the row.

'Bloody typical.'

She shoved the paper back in her pocket, cursed the mud that was clinging to her shoes, and rummaged in her bag.

As she approached the last narrowboat, she ran her gaze over the dull blue paint around the windows and the worn timber gunwales.

A figure stood on the stern, coiling a rope, his head

bowed as he worked. Dark curly hair lifted on the breeze as he turned away from her and threw something on the deck, a soft thud reaching her ears.

He wore a navy sweatshirt and jeans, his feet covered by boots that appeared to have seen better days. The sort that Scott would call his "gardening boots" whenever she suggested throwing them away.

Before she could open her mouth and call out to him, a dog barked. A split second later, a dark shape launched itself from another boat at her.

'Hamish, no!'

The man's voice carried across to the animal too late to save the hem of her trousers. Muddy paw prints soon peppered the charcoal-grey material, and she groaned.

'Come here!'

The dog trotted off towards the narrowboat, the man's voice sounding more amused than cross to her ears.

He straightened as she drew near, a frown creasing his brow while he kept his fingers looped through the dog's collar.

'Can I help you?'

She took a deep breath. 'Detective Sergeant Mark Turpin?'

'Who are you?'

She held up her warrant card. 'I'm Detective Constable Jan West. There's been a murder, and the guv needs you at the crime scene.'

CHAPTER THREE

'Why rent a boat, not a house?'

'There was nothing else available at short notice. I figured I'd rent it for six months while I scout around for something more permanent.'

Mark moved through the narrow wooden cabin, shedding his walking boots and sweatshirt while trying to continue the conversation with the detective constable.

He could hear her on the other side of the minuscule window, hovering on the shallow deck while she waited, her heels clomping on the wooden surface every few seconds as her shadow passed across the net curtain.

'I'd never have thought to rent a boat,' she said.

'It was easy. I made some phone calls, introduced

myself to a few of the regulars at the marina in town, and signed the lease three weeks ago.'

'Why don't you moor closer to town? It'd be easier to get to.'

'That's the whole idea. It's not easy to get to. I need peace and quiet.'

He balanced on one foot and removed his jeans, knocking his elbow against the timber-panelled wall before opening the single cupboard that served as his wardrobe and tugged a pair of black trousers off a plastic hanger. The movement sent it clanging against the back of the wardrobe, echoing off the walls.

'Won't it be cold in the winter?' said Jan. 'I can't see a chimney like your neighbour's boat has.'

'It's only temporary. I plan to move into a house before it gets too cold. Anyway, lots of people live on narrowboats, don't they?'

A shirt hung over the back of a chair next to the window, and he snatched it up, holding it to his nose for a moment.

It would have to do.

'What about all your stuff?'

'Storage place on the outskirts of town.' He grimaced. 'Costs a fortune.'

He hopped about, pulling on a pair of smart black boots he'd found on sale in a shop in Oxford prior to his formal interview. That done, he reached out for a jacket he'd left lying on the duvet, and made his way along the main cabin while he secured a tie under his shirt collar, past the boxes that lined the seats each side and filled the galley, and pushed open the door.

Jan was standing with her back to him, tying her mid-length brown hair into a neat bun at the nape of her neck. She turned at the sound of the cabin door closing and dropped her hands to her sides, green eyes appraising him.

'Ready?' she said.

'Yes.'

She jerked her attention over her shoulder to where Hamish was on his back in the grass, his tongue lolling. 'You should keep your dog under control, by the way.'

'He's not my dog.'

'What do you mean?'

'He turned up on the towpath one day and jumped on board. I've got no idea where he's from.'

'Hasn't anyone been looking for him?'

'No.' He leapt from the deck in one long stride.

'Oh.' She reached out to steady herself as the boat rocked. 'That's sad, isn't it? What sort of dog is he?'

'I don't know. A mongrel, I suppose – a bit of Schnauzer, a bit of terrier, and a bit of something else.'

She didn't answer, and when he glanced over his

shoulder, he noticed she had climbed off the boat and onto the towpath, a look of unease on her face.

'Aren't you going to lock it?'

'No, it'll be fine. Lucy next door will keep an eye on it for me.'

He bit back a smile as she cast a glance at the narrowboat next to his, its decorations of wind chimes, bright flowerpots and hanging baskets contrasting strikingly with his own boat.

After a moment she shrugged as if she couldn't care less if his home got broken into because he'd ignored her advice and preferred to let a hippy guard it.

'Come on then. They're waiting for us.'

He inhaled the aroma of wet earth as they walked along the grassy bank, his ears picking up the faint splash of a vole entering the water at the sound of their voices.

Concentric circles appeared on the surface of the water a moment before bubbles escaped, and he noted with interest the faint outline of a trout as it made its way across to the other bank.

He had hoped to take advantage of another week off work to get used to his new environment and settle in, but it seemed a killer had other ideas about his brief sabbatical.

'You didn't hear a word I said, did you?'

He glanced at Jan, to find her glaring at him. 'Sorry, what?'

'When are they going to give you a mobile phone?'

'I don't know. I wasn't meant to start for another week. I suppose I'll get kitted out with everything then. Why?'

'Well, it'd be easier getting hold of you. No-one could find your personal number.'

He reached out with his hand to steady her as she slipped in the mud. 'Didn't you grow up in the countryside around here?'

Her mouth quirked. 'Is it that obvious? No, I'm a city girl – sort of. I moved up here from Exeter when I was sixteen.'

'Tell me what you know about the murder,' he said. He dropped his hand once he was sure she wasn't going to fall over, and then let her walk on ahead as the path narrowed.

She began to move away, and called over her shoulder.

'It's a priest, apparently. Killed in his own church. Pathologist and CSIs are already on site.'

'Location?'

'Upper Benham. Do you know it?'

'Not well. I only arrived here recently. I know the towns and larger villages around here, but you're going to have to bear with me while I learn the smaller ones.'

'You were based in Wiltshire before coming here, weren't you?'

'Yeah.'

'Well, it won't take you long to fit in. It's a friendly place.'

'Apart from someone murdering the local priest, you mean?'

He smiled at the snort of laughter that emanated from the detective in front of him.

They hurried along in silence, the long grass smacking against the hem of his trousers and the sound of water lapping against the riverbank receding as they passed the cottages.

Jan strode on ahead, the path narrowing on each side, and he wondered how she managed to walk in the shoes she was wearing, not surprised she was sliding all over the place.

'Do you own a pair of boots, Jan?'

'Pardon?'

'Boots. Might be more suitable than those for work.'

'Thanks, Sarge. I'll bear that in mind. I was meant to be off duty today when I got the call. They didn't tell me my new DS lives on a boat in the middle of the bloody river.'

She stomped off, and he swore under his breath as he hurried to catch up.

'Who found the body?'

'The church sacristan. Gave her a right shock, I'll bet.'

'First on scene?'

'Local patrol. They got there within twenty minutes of control getting the triple nine call. Apparently, they'd been on duty all night and were returning to base when it came through.'

'Catholic, or Church of England?'

She stopped in her tracks and turned to face him, one hand on the metal gate. 'Catholic, but does it matter right now? He's dead anyway.'

He squinted through the cool morning sunlight at the boats in the distance, then back to her. 'No, I suppose not.'

'Right then. Car's over here.'

CHAPTER FOUR

A gust of wind sent white clouds scudding across a pale-blue sky and buffeted the pool car.

Jan reached out and adjusted the heat setting, the interior of the car warming as the late spring morning developed into what Mark expected of an early day in May.

Apart from the murder of a parish priest.

'What do you know about the victim?'

His hand shot out, seeking the strap above the passenger door as Jan powered the car around a tight bend. The door mirror clipped a hawthorn bush as they passed and scared a brightly coloured pheasant that ran squawking under a five-bar gate on the opposite side of the lane.

'Seamus Carter. The church sacristan, Helen,

found him. He's been the parish priest for about fifteen years. He was expected to arrive at the church a couple of hours before the Pentecost service this morning. He'd arranged for her to get there first, so she could check over the flower arrangements and deal with any last-minute food donations for the charity baskets. When she got there, the church was already unlocked, and she discovered his body in the vestry.'

'Just to be clear, which part of the building is the vestry?'

'At the back. Typically used as an office, as well as a place for the priest to get ready before a service. Haven't you ever been to church?'

'Not since I got married, no.'

'Oh.'

He rubbed his thumb over the space where the wedding band used to be, then shuffled in his seat and peered through the window as she indicated left and powered the car towards the village.

Mark ran his eyes over the sign welcoming them to Upper Benham, then let his gaze travel over the sight of a village green bordered by a post office and a duck pond.

The church tower could be seen above a row of horse chestnut trees.

As the car drew closer, he noted a long wall

separating the church from a pub, a stile cut into the stonework so that walkers could access the footpath that bisected the properties.

He was pleased to see that the entrance to the church grounds had been cordoned off by the first responders. Blue and white tape fluttered between two gate posts, and now a small crowd of churchgoers huddled together as uniformed officers corralled them away from the crime scene in order to take statements.

The state of shock was palpable, and officers moved between the men and women that were gathered, notebooks poised to get as much information down as possible from each individual before the parishioners had too much of a chance to talk to each other and clouded their own recall of events.

Jan braked next to a plain white panel van and killed the engine. 'Shit.'

'Something wrong?'

She pointed at the sleek black four-door car that had been parked further up the lane from their position.

'The Home Office pathologist is still here.'

'What's wrong with that?'

His colleague sighed. 'She's incredibly clever, and good at what she does – she just isn't very patient with those of us with an inability to keep up with her.'

'What's her name?'

'Gillian Appleworth.'

Mark emitted a groan.

'What's the matter?' said Jan.

He didn't answer, and instead unclipped his seatbelt and flung open the door.

Jan at his side, he stalked across the road to where a white tent had been erected. He pushed aside the flap and took two sets of white overalls from the crime scene technician, pulling one set over his suit and stepping into the matching booties while his colleague did the same. After signing in with the police officer who stood guard outside the church entrance, he turned to the detective constable.

'Have you done this before?'

'Now and then, if I'm on duty at the time,' she said, adjusting the hood over her hair. 'An old lady got bashed in her home about six months ago on the outskirts of Didcot. Not nice.'

'I hate to say it, but I think this one is going to be worse.'

She paled at his words, but he noticed how she braced her shoulders before following him.

The double doors to the church had been pegged open, providing ease of access to the crime scene investigators and police officers that were milling about.

A familiar mustiness filled his senses as he passed under the porch and into the building.

Dust motes hung in the air, spiralling in the light cast through the stained glass windows. A demarcated path had been set out using tape, and two crime scene investigators worked on the far side of the church. One raised a digital camera, the bright flash illuminating the plasterwork wall as another paced back and forth, his head bowed.

'Do you know if there was any sign of a forced entry?'

'The first responders reported that the sacristan said there wasn't,' said Jan. 'There are two entrances into the church, and both were open – the front door we just came through, and a side door that leads out to the car park.'

Mark paused, and craned his neck until he could look at the ceiling above. Lights hung from long cords that dangled from pale oak rafters, the glow from the bulbs casting a soft hue across the large space.

'So, I wonder if our killer entered the building earlier in the day and waited?'

Jan shook her head. 'Helen Wilson, that's the sacristan, said they had a busy day yesterday – a wedding in the morning, and a christening in the afternoon. Once those were out of the way, the priest and the ushers prepared the church for the service that was going to be held this morning.'

'Are you religious?'

'Not particularly, Sarge. No.'

'Then why are you whispering?'

'I don't know. Isn't that what people usually do in churches?'

He turned on his heel and led the way towards the back of the church where two figures in similar white overalls to theirs hovered next to a doorway, their attention taken by the activities beyond.

The nearest turned at the sound of their footsteps, and lowered his paper mask as they approached.

'DS Mark Turpin. I believe you know DC Jan West. Detective Inspector Kennedy is managing the incident room being established at Abingdon, and I'm attending as his deputy Senior Investigating Officer.'

'Lucky you. Come through. The pathologist and CSI lead are here.'

The man replaced his mask, and stepped aside to let them pass.

Inside, two identically white-suited figures spoke in hushed tones near the back wall of the room while bending over a chair and a desk, their feet on a raised platform that had been erected.

Mark didn't need to ask why – a pool of blood had congealed across the tiled floor.

The room looked as if it had been used as an office for a number of years. Two metal filing cabinets had been placed beside the desk, their drawers unopened. The walls were sparsely decorated. A wooden crucifix adorned the space above them, and a calendar hung from a hook driven into the wall on the right-hand side, its page turned to May and displaying a photograph of the Uffington White Horse above a field of wheat.

Neither person paid any attention to the new arrivals, and remained focused on the task at hand.

Mark cleared his throat. 'Right, what have we got?'

The figure in the white overalls on the left spun around, the space between the hood and a face mask revealing cool grey eyes that bored into his a moment as he heard her sharp intake of breath.

'Mark? I'd heard you'd relocated this way.'

'Gillian.'

'Oh, do you know each other?' said Jan.

'You could say that,' said the pathologist. She stepped off the platform and gestured to her left. 'Stay on that side of the room, next to the wall. They've finished processing that area.'

Mark led the way, the paper soles of his bootees scuffing over the mottled flagstones.

Despite the animosity between him and Gillian Appleworth, he respected her work ethic and he could see why she was determined to keep a safe distance from where she and the team of CSIs worked.

The slumped body of the priest sat hunched forwards in a plain wooden chair, his back to the room, one arm dangling at his side while the other rested on the table in front of him.

His thin brown hair exposed a pale scalp, a navy wool sweater covering his slim shoulders. Blood covered the wall above him, a wide arc that had hit the wall and splashed outwards, coating a laptop computer, paperwork and leather briefcase – as well as the lower half of the cross nailed to the wall.

Mark frowned. 'What happened?'

Gillian paused from speaking with one of the technicians and glanced over her shoulder at him.

'He was attacked from behind – a rope was used to restrain him by the neck while his tongue was removed. The attacker then slit his throat.'

He heard Jan swallow before she spoke.

'He was alive when his tongue was cut out?'

'Quite possibly. We haven't found it yet, so he might've been made to swallow it.'

'Did no-one hear?'

'No.' The pathologist pointed at the laptop. 'This was blasting out classical music when the first responders got here, and apparently the pub next door had a live band last night.'

'Any fingerprints?'

Another figure clad in white overalls turned and shook his head. 'We might have some partials, but whoever did this wore thin gloves – enough to mask any prints at least.'

'What about a weapon?' said Mark.

'No sign of one, nor the rope that was used to wrap around his neck.'

'Definitely a rope?'

Gillian threw him a withering look and cocked her head to one side as she appraised him. 'The ligature marks are quite distinctive, Detective Turpin. We have photos. I'm sure we'll be able to tell you the exact kind of rope that was used once we've had time to analyse those and retrieve any trace fibres from the wound.'

'No footprints?' said Jan.

'He was attacked from behind. The blood arced away from the killer so, no – no footprints. We checked outside, too, but found no markings on the surface of the car park.'

'That took a hell of a lot of strength,' said Mark, and jerked his chin at the priest's prone body. 'He's not a small man.'

'Factor in anger, blood lust or anything like that, and you'd be surprised what people are capable of. You must've seen what people are like when they're fired up and ready to fight.'

'Male or female?'

'I couldn't comment. However, it took a certain amount of strength to overpower him.' Gillian gestured to a collection of paperwork that lay scattered around the victim's feet, as if they had been swept off the desk during a struggle. 'Looks like he tried to defend himself. There are traces of rope fibres under his fingernails as well.'

'Fat lot of good it did him,' said Mark. 'All right, we'll let you get on. When do you think you could have your preliminary report to us?'

'When it's ready.'

He sighed as the pathologist turned her back on him once more, and then led the way from the vestry, Jan at his heels.

They reached the exit, and he took in a deep lungful of air, keen to lose the scent of blood from his nostrils before he stalked across to the tent and removed the overalls.

He straightened and noticed Jan talking to one of the police constables on the cordon, a smile on her lips as she tossed the car keys from hand to hand.

She noticed him approaching, and broke off her conversation as she headed back towards the car.

'What are you grinning about?'

She waited until he'd fallen into step beside her.

'So, Nathan over there says that the pathologist is your ex-wife's sister?'

He sighed, marvelling at the speed at which news travelled within the police force. 'It's complicated.'

'No kidding.'

CHAPTER FIVE

Jan attempted a shortcut back to town, but got caught in gridlocked traffic once they reached the outskirts of Abingdon.

She swore under her breath as the car crawled forward behind an articulated truck, and flexed her fingers around the steering wheel.

Beside her, Turpin stared out of the window as if lost in thought, and she wondered if she was going to be lumbered with the new detective, or whether she could hand him over to an unsuspecting DC McClellan upon reaching the police station.

She had heard a new detective sergeant would be joining the team based at the station but had expected someone local to be deployed – someone familiar with the area, at least.

Now, on top of what would be a high-profile

murder investigation for the major crimes team, they would have to adjust to a stranger in their midst.

She wondered why he had the voice of a smoker – she hadn't seen him reach into his jacket pocket for a cigarette in the short time they'd been together, and his clothes didn't reek of smoke.

As she shot him a sideways glance, she decided to single out one of her colleagues when she could, and find out what they knew about DS Mark Turpin.

Braking to a standstill, she wound down her window, swiped her security card across a panel fixed next to a metal sliding gate, and then drove into the car park behind the police station.

Detective Inspector Kennedy's car was in its usual spot under one of the CCTV cameras. Considering that he worked in one of the larger local policing area's stations, he remained paranoid that someone would damage or steal his car. Jan had heard that he had spent a considerable amount of money and several years restoring the classic MG, and couldn't help wondering why he simply didn't buy something newer that didn't break down all the time.

She aimed the key fob at the car, and then led the way into the building.

'I'll have to sign you in until they can sort you out with your own swipe card.'

Jan waited while the sergeant behind the front

desk arranged for a visitor pass card for Turpin, then pushed through a metal security gate and led the way towards the lift.

He fell into step beside her, and then tapped her arm and pointed at the stairs.

'Do you mind if we take these instead? I wouldn't mind stretching my legs after the car ride.'

She hesitated, and then shrugged. 'Okay.'

She wondered if she had been lumbered with a health freak the way he bounded up the stairs in front of her, and resisted the urge to groan. By the time she reached the second level, she was out of breath. She had been so busy at work the past six weeks, she'd neglected her exercise routine, and resolved to go for a swim on the way home. If she tried to do anything after walking through her front door, it would be impossible – Harry and Luke would want their dinner, and Scott would hand her a glass of wine.

She managed a smile at Turpin as she caught up with him, and then headed down the corridor to the incident room, pushing through the door into a cacophony of activity.

On any typical working day, there would be a core team of detective constables and sergeants on hand to deal with criminal investigations in the area.

Except, this wasn't a typical working day. Despite it being a Sunday, the brutal slaying of a priest had put paid to that. Hence the presence of Detective Inspector Ewan Kennedy, who barked orders from the front of the room, sweat patches pooling under his arms as he directed his team and began the long process of leading a murder enquiry.

She had worked with him once before, and knew that beneath his gruff exterior was a man of grim determination and fairness. She might not always agree with him, but his reputation was one of the most respected.

He glanced up from a sheaf of papers in his hand as she approached and peered over his reading glasses. 'You found my new DS then, Jan?'

'Guv. We've just got back from the crime scene.'

'Is it as bad as I've heard?'

'Yes. Nasty.' She turned and gestured to Turpin, formally introducing the two men.

'Sorry your sabbatical ended early, Mark. Your predecessor moved on a month ago, leaving us short-staffed, and I need someone with your experience to be my deputy SIO.'

The newcomer shrugged. 'It was only by a matter of days, guv. Given the circumstances, it's not a problem.'

'Good man. Before you ask, Jan, I've already approved overtime for you.'

'You're a legend, guv – thanks.'

Kennedy turned his attention to the other occupants in the room, and raised his voice. 'Right, you lot. Now that we're all here, let's have a quick recap of events to date, and then we'll go through initial tasks for today.'

Jan observed how Turpin gravitated towards the edge of the circle of police officers who gathered next to a whiteboard Kennedy began to write on.

She wondered why he had been on a sabbatical in the first place, then turned her attention to the DI as he began the briefing.

'This is what we know so far. Seamus Carter was the parish priest at the Catholic Church in Upper Benham,' he said. 'Fifty-six, lives alone in the village and, according to the woman who's the sacristan from the church, Helen Wilson, he wouldn't hurt a fly. His murder was, as Jan observed earlier, nasty. Attacked while working in his office at the church, the pathologist has confirmed that he was restrained from behind using a rope that was placed around his neck before his tongue was cut out. His throat was then slit in such a way that he was nearly decapitated.'

He paused and pinned three photographs to the whiteboard, and then consulted his notes once more. 'The church shares a boundary with the local pub, the White Horse. The pub holds a live music event every Saturday night, and witness statements are being collated from those who attended last night's gig. House-to-house enquiries are continuing this morning, and the HOLMES2 database will be updated with all those statements over the course of the next twenty-four hours.'

Jan watched as Turpin took notes, his head bowed and his brow furrowed in concentration. Compared to two of the other detectives that hovered next to him, he seemed unflustered by the number of tasks that were being delegated throughout the team, as if he had experienced a similar major incident all too often.

She forced herself to concentrate at the sound of her name.

'Jan – I'd like you to accompany Mark and go to the priest's house while CSI are conducting their search there this morning, then go and interview Helen Wilson. Obviously, she's distraught. She's already provided the first responders with a statement but hopefully once she's had a chance to calm down, she might be able to provide us with more information.'

Once Kennedy had finished the debrief, the team began to disperse.

Jan saw a familiar figure pushing between the desks to reach her, and beckoned Turpin over as the man approached.

She wished the newcomer didn't look quite so suave – notwithstanding his hurried exodus from his home on the water that morning, he still managed to make the rest of them appear scruffy, none more so than her young colleague who hovered expectantly, waiting for an introduction while he tucked his shirt into the waistband of his trousers.

She suppressed a sigh.

'Mark, this is Detective Constable—'

The man sneezed, spluttering over his fingers before wiping his hand on his trousers and then extending it to Turpin. 'Sorry – hay fever. I'm Alex McClellan.'

CHAPTER SIX

Jan rummaged in her handbag and extracted two foil-wrapped parcels, handing one to Turpin as they walked towards a silver coloured car.

'What's this?'

'Cheese and pickle.'

He looked at her with amusement. 'Do you have kids?'

'Two boys. Both with hollow legs.'

'I can tell. Thank you.'

Reaching the vehicle, she unlocked it and placed her bag on the roof before tearing open the foil.

Turpin leaned against the car, and followed suit. 'What does your husband do?'

'Scott? He's a painter and decorator. Been doing it since he was a teenager, and now runs his own business. Has two or three blokes working for him,

NONE THE WISER   39

depending how much they've got on. And he's always home by four o'clock in the afternoon, so there's someone there for the boys if I'm busy.'

'Sounds like it works out great for you all.'

She smiled. 'It does, yeah. Have you got kids?'

'Two daughters, twelve and fourteen,' he said, a warmth in his voice. 'They live with their mum back in Swindon.'

'Oh. Do you get to see much of them?'

'Every fortnight, depending on work. It is what it is,' he said between mouthfuls. 'How long have you been based here?'

'About four years. Before that, I was based out of Newbury. This is better, though. Easier with the kids.' She peered through the car window, and swallowed. 'Oh, bloody hell.'

'What's wrong?'

'Tracy has given us the car that Alex was using this morning.'

'Is there a problem?'

She didn't answer, and instead aimed the key fob at it, then opened her bag and withdrew a plastic carrier bag with a supermarket logo emblazoned across the sides.

As Turpin opened the passenger door, she proceeded to pick up the empty sandwich wrappers and other litter from the back of the vehicle, placing everything into the bag and then shoving it behind the driver's seat.

That done, she got in and started the engine. She turned to check over her shoulder as she began to reverse the car out of the space, and saw Turpin watching her, a look of bemusement on his face as he fished an empty soft drink can from the footwell and added it to the bag.

'Don't worry, I'll be having a word with him,' she said.

They were underway and heading in the direction of Upper Benham before Turpin spoke again.

'How long has McClellan been a DC?'

She shrugged. 'Not long. He joined us from Bicester six months ago after completing his probationary period.'

'Does he own a comb?'

She laughed. 'He might be a slob and a bit wet behind the ears, but he's got the makings of a good detective, Sarge.'

'He looks like he's been dragged through a hedge backwards. Twice.'

———————

JAN APPLIED the handbrake and peered through the

windscreen at the compact brick detached house that had once been the home of Seamus Carter.

At some point over the years, ugly pebbledash had been applied to the walls, giving the whole building a dirty off-grey appearance. The original frames had been replaced with UPVC, no doubt in an attempt to weatherproof the building.

She climbed out of the vehicle and joined Turpin on the threshold.

He peered through the open front door and gave a low whistle.

'Hang on.'

A rustling sound emanated from a door off to the right of where they stood, and then a tall figure encased in white protective clothing with a mask over his face appeared. The skin around his eyes crinkled when he caught sight of her, and he lowered his mask.

'January West. Who's your new sidekick?'

She ignored the sideways glance her new DS threw her way at the use of her full name, and provided the introductions instead.

Jasper Smith nodded in greeting, and held up his gloved hands. 'Welcome. I'd shake your hand but—'

'No problem,' said Turpin. 'Mind if we have a look around?'

'Not at all – we're nearly finished. Here, put on some overalls.'

Jan took one set of the coveralls that the CSI lead handed out, then placed her bag next to the doorway and removed her shoes before pulling the white suit over her clothes. After tying plastic booties over the top of her shoes, she followed Jasper and Turpin into the house.

'Anything of significance?' said Turpin over her shoulder.

'The place is quite sparse – through there is the living room, you've got three bedrooms upstairs, and a kitchen at the back of the house. He's been using one of the bedrooms as his office, and that's where most of our time has been taken up. We've got diaries for the past four years, and there's a whole filing cabinet full of official stuff. But, no sign of a break-in at any time, and his car keys are on a hook in the kitchen. There's a garage down the side of the property, and the car is in there. The tank is three quarters full, and it looks in good condition considering its age.'

Jan let Smith's voice wash over her as she wandered through the house in his wake, her eyes absorbing what had been the priest's life away from his church.

As they entered the living room, she was struck by the plain decor. A dark-green emulsion paint had been applied to the walls, contrasting with the off-white ceiling. On one wall, a watercolour painting of the village hung above an ancient television set. Bookshelves lined the opposite wall behind a three-seater sofa that sat in front of a low coffee table. A coffee stain covered the left-hand corner, next to which a selection of parish leaflets curled with age.

'Did he have a cleaner?' said Turpin.

'Priests usually live alone, Sarge,' she said. 'He would have been responsible for his own shopping, cooking, and cleaning the house in between his parish duties.'

She was suddenly thankful that she hadn't had to bring McClellan here – he would have made a flippant comment about the priest's life, and laughed or joked about something wholly inappropriate.

Instead, the new DS ran a gloved hand over the dead priest's belongings with reverence, taking care to replace items as he had found them, and followed Smith in silence as he led them through the rest of the house.

When they reached the top of the stairs, Smith gestured to an open doorway beyond the bathroom.

'That's his office – we've finished in there, so it's all yours. The diaries are on the desk if you want to take a look before we box them up. There's an address book as well. I'll be downstairs completing the search of the garage if you need me.'

Turpin nodded his thanks, and then stepped to one side to let Jan into the room ahead of him.

Immediately, she could see why the priest had chosen the room as his office.

The window overlooked a garden and a shed-like structure to the left of the house, which was obviously the garage, given the three CSIs that wandered back and forth from it. Beyond the garden, open fields stretched away from the village, leading towards a copse of trees on the near horizon.

Seamus Carter had placed his desk directly under the window, and she could imagine him gazing out across the landscape as he contemplated his work.

'Interesting.'

She turned at Turpin's voice. 'What is?'

He pointed at the top-of-the-range computer set to the right-hand side of the desk. 'Everything we've seen here so far has been older models of things – the television downstairs, for example. And Smith said that Carter's car is good for its age too. And yet, both the laptop at the church and this one is new.'

'Technology freak?'

'Maybe.' Turpin turned his attention to the A4-sized diaries that Smith and his team had bagged up and left on the desk for collection once they had concluded their search. 'The minute these have been logged by the exhibits officer back at the incident room,

NONE THE WISER   45

we'll get uniform to go through them – hopefully there's something in there that will help us.'

She paused while he reached out and ran his hand over the books on the shelf next to the desk before turning back to her.

'It seems a lonely existence for a man otherwise surrounded by people, doesn't it?'

CHAPTER SEVEN

Jan jabbed her foot on the brake pedal and cursed as a kid on a pushbike sneered at her and then weaved between two parked cars on the side of the street and disappeared from sight.

'Little toe rag.'

'Do you know him?' Turpin glanced up from his notes and peered through the windscreen.

'Only by sight. He used to live up past the Oxford Road. Got done for shoplifting a while ago.'

'How old are your kids?'

'Twins. Eight, going on eighteen.'

She shoved the car into gear and set off once more, accelerating once they'd passed the turning for the main road.

'Do your boys go to the same school as him?'

'What? No – they're too young. Anyway, by the time they're his age, they'll be at the boys' school.'

Turpin twisted in his seat. 'I sense a hint of stress there, Jan.'

She acknowledged his words by wrinkling her nose, changing gear as countryside replaced urban sprawl. 'I don't want my two to go to the secondary school, all right? I'm worried they'll get bullied by the likes of him.'

'So, what – public school, is it?'

'Exactly.'

'On a copper's wage?' He chuckled. 'Not up to something dodgy, are you?'

She bit her lip.

His laughter subsided. 'Jan?'

She sighed, then indicated left and took a winding route towards the opposite end of Upper Benham.

On any other day, she'd have marvelled at the change in the surrounding countryside. An unforgiving winter had given way to a rain-drenched spring that brought grey skies and flooded roads that caused treacherous conditions across the local policing area.

Now, an overcast morning had turned tail for the Berkshire Downs, leaving behind a bright sunshine-soaked landscape of fields and hedgerows with a tantalising glimpse of warmer weather only weeks away.

'Jan?'

'Look, it's like this. There are scholarships, okay?'

'Oh, right.' He sat back in his seat for a moment, and then out of the corner of her eye, she watched his brow furrow. 'What sort of scholarships?'

She took a deep breath. 'Music. If they can demonstrate a certain level of competency over the next eighteen months or so, then they might be in with a chance of getting in. The scholarships cover sixty per cent of the costs.'

Turpin gave a low whistle. 'Nice work. What instrument?'

'Trombone.'

'What—'

His response was cut off as he snorted at the same time, and she was rewarded with the sound of his spluttering from the passenger seat.

He beat at his chest, and after a startled glance across to make sure he wasn't choking, she felt her shoulders relax as a smile tugged at the side of her mouth.

'It's not funny, Sarge.'

'My God, but it is,' he wheezed. 'Twin boys, and they're both learning trombone. I can imagine the racket.'

'They're actually quite good.'

'Is this why Kennedy told you he'd already

approved your overtime for this case, to save you hearing it?'

'Okay, yes – I'll admit it's good to come to work to get away from the noise sometimes.'

He stopped laughing, as if picking up on her change of tone. 'But it'll get them into the school they want, right?'

'Exactly. The deal is, once they're in they can pick whatever instrument they like.'

'Only another eighteen months to go, then?'

'Only eighteen months.'

'You'd better hope they don't want to learn the drums next.'

She clenched her jaw while he wiped at his eyes and tried to compose himself, then slowed the car, and pointed to the house opposite.

'We're here.'

She shut her car door and stalked across the lane towards the terraced cottage.

'Jan. Wait.'

He caught up with her, buttoning his jacket, then reached out and pulled her to a stop on the pavement.

'I won't say another word about it. I can see how much it means to you to get your boys into the right school.'

'Thanks.'

He nodded, then turned his attention to the gabled house and ran his eyes over the façade.

'She's doing all right for herself, helping out at a church.'

'The officers who took her statement this morning said her husband died two years ago. Heart attack. Completely out of the blue, apparently. He was a board member of a city firm for a number of years, made some sensible investment choices, left his wife with a house that had been completely paid off, and a nice monthly income from the share portfolio.'

Turpin narrowed his eyes. 'Makes you wonder why she needs a job at the church then, doesn't it?'

'It's voluntary, Sarge. She doesn't get paid.'

By the time she had finished speaking, he had already cleared the three shallow steps to the cottage's front garden and rapped on the door.

She trotted after him, reaching the coir mat on the front step as the door opened and red-rimmed eyes peered out at them. She was surprised at the woman's appearance. She had expected an older woman, but guessed that Helen was only in her late fifties.

She wore black jeans and a cream-coloured cashmere sweater, her dark brown hair kept at shoulder length.

The sweet aroma of fresh baking wafted over the

threshold, and Jan gritted her teeth as her stomach threatened to rumble.

'Mrs Wilson?' Turpin introduced them both, then patted the outside of his jacket and frowned before turning back to Jan. 'Have you got some business cards?'

She nodded, rummaged in her handbag, and held out a dog-eared card to the woman.

'I spoke to the police this morning,' said Helen as she peered at Jan's credentials.

'I appreciate that, but I've been appointed as the deputy Senior Investigating Officer on this case,' said Turpin, 'and it's usual for us to speak to witnesses as well in these sorts of circumstances.'

The woman stepped to one side and held open the door for them.

'You had better come in, then. I suppose you want tea.'

Turpin stepped over the threshold after wiping his feet on the mat, leaving Jan to close the door.

'Only if you're having one.'

The woman didn't reply, and instead led them through a narrow hallway to the kitchen at the back of the cottage that had been extended out from the original floor plan.

A six-seater dining table had been placed at the far end next to a window seat that provided a reading nook overlooking the garden. The property backed onto fields, a lone tractor passing the barbed wire fence along the boundary as it rumbled across the landscape.

Two wire cooling racks sat on a worktop next to the oven, with neat rows of cupcakes lined beside the beginnings of a sponge pudding.

'That smells wonderful,' said Jan.

'I find it relaxing,' said Helen as she began to tidy and stack bowls in a dishwasher. 'I didn't know what else to do. I sometimes bake for fundraisers in the village but it's not like it was years ago. The food safety rules are a nuisance – it puts a lot of people off from helping out these days.'

Helen placed a stainless steel kettle on the stove and lit the gas, then turned to the two detectives. She gestured to the dining table, and joined them as they took their seats. 'Anyway, you're not here to talk about that, are you?'

'Are you here on your own?' said Turpin. 'Do you have a friend or family member who can be with you at this time?'

Helen shook her head. 'I have friends in the village I can call if I need them later.'

Jan pulled out her notebook from her bag and uncapped a pen.

'Can you take me through the events of this

morning?' said Turpin. 'I realise this is very traumatic for you, but it's essential to our enquiries.'

The woman nodded, and sniffed. 'It's one of the busiest days of the year for us. We had set up almost everything yesterday after the christening, but I arranged with Father Carter to come in early today to check the flower arrangements and help him get ready before the congregation began to arrive.'

'What time did you get to the church?'

'About seven o'clock, I think.'

'Did you drive, walk—'

'I drove. I had the boxes of cleaning stuff with me, and it's too bulky to carry that far.'

The kettle began to whistle, and she pushed herself up from her chair, fussed around selecting cups for them, and then set down a tray on the table.

'Help yourself to milk and sugar.'

Jan tipped a splash of milk into her mug, and noted that Turpin did the same – no sugar.

He picked up a spoon and stirred his drink before turning his attention back to Helen.

'How long have you worked at the church?'

'Two years.'

'Seamus Carter had been in the area for nearly fifteen years – what happened to the last sacristan?'

'She retired. Mary O'Brien was her name. Even after she stopped working there, she still attended Mass every Sunday until she died about eight months ago. She had an enormous stroke, and because she lived on her own, she didn't receive help in time.'

'I'm sorry to hear that.' Turpin paused, and took a sip of tea. 'Why do you work at the church?'

'What do you mean?'

'Do you need the money?'

'It doesn't pay, detective. It's a voluntary role. And, I don't need the money – when my husband died, he left me with enough insurance cover to pay off the mortgage. He was a wise man, detective. He invested well, and I'm grateful for that.'

'So, why the part-time job at the church?'

She set down a cup of tea, her features clouding. 'Because I'm lonely. I only learned to drive after Derek died, and I'm not that confident. Yes, I can drive around the village and I can get to the supermarket and back without any trouble, but it's not like I'm going gallivanting around now that he's gone. Besides, I like to help.'

'Do you socialise much in the village?'

'I didn't, until recently. As you can imagine, it took me a long time to get through everything when I lost my husband. I miss him dreadfully. But a couple of friends from the church and I have gone out for a drink at the pub a few times in the past three or four months, and I've started taking art classes once a week at the church hall.'

'Back to this morning. What happened when you arrived at the church?'

'When I got there, the door was open – I mean although it had been closed, it wasn't locked. I called out to Father Carter, but there was no answer. The lights were still on, well some of them, anyway. It looked as if they'd been left on from last night. I couldn't see him anywhere in the church, so I made my way through to the office thinking he'd be there—' She brought a shaking hand to her mouth, and closed her eyes. 'There was so much blood.'

Jan fought down her own memories of the crime scene, and noted how patiently Turpin waited while Helen composed herself.

Eventually, the woman opened her eyes and hugged herself. She blinked.

'What did you do?' said Turpin, his voice calm.

'Obviously I realised he was dead – and I've watched enough television to know I shouldn't touch anything. I felt sick. I ran outside, and managed to get to the car park before I threw up. I still had my handbag with me and my phone, and that's when I phoned nine-nine-nine.'

'Had Seamus argued with anyone recently, do you know?'

She sighed, leaned forward, and clasped her hands together on the table. 'I know he and Terry, who owns the pub, had a slight altercation last month – it's the car parking, you see. The pub and the church share an easement, and there's a footpath that runs between the church and the pub car park. There's some sort of by-law that stipulates that no vehicles should block the footpath at any time, but often people will leave their cars behind and walk home if they've had too much to drink, and then of course they're late picking them up the next day, so people can't use the footpath to get to the church for Sunday Mass. I can't believe Terry would harm Father Carter over that though, not like that. What was done to Seamus was the work of evil.'

CHAPTER EIGHT

Mark thanked Helen, then hurried down the footpath to where Jan stood next to the car, her forehead lined with concentration.

'Where to next, Sarge?'

'The pub, I think. Let's find out how much of an "altercation" our church priest had with the publican last month.'

He climbed in, and buckled his seatbelt as she started the engine.

'I can't imagine an argument over an easement would be bad enough to give him a motive for murder.'

'Me neither, but we need to rule it out.'

He peered out of the window as she steered the car along the winding lane from Helen's house and took a right-hand turn that led them through the main part of the village.

The church and pub were at the far end, and as they progressed through Upper Benham, he noted the village store and post office maintained a thriving trade – no doubt helped by gossip about the priest's death that morning.

He watched a group of people gathered on the pavement outside the shop, and wondered if Carter's murderer was amongst them. Pale faces stared at him as the car passed, and he turned his attention back to Jan.

'Do you know this place at all?'

'Upper Benham?'

'Yeah.'

She shrugged. 'Not well. I think we've driven through it a few times on our way to Wallingford, but we've never stopped. I've never really taken any notice of it until now.'

'Typical sleepy village, then?'

'I checked the database after this morning's briefing. Apart from a couple of minor break-ins a few years ago, there's nothing. Picture-perfect, you could say.'

He grunted under his breath as she steered the vehicle around the picturesque duck pond, three white ducks bobbing around on the water's surface in the middle. Wooden benches had been erected on the grass verges next to the pond, but were currently abandoned. He imagined that at weekends the space would be filled with families having picnics.

He turned his attention to a building facing the duck pond, and realised as he ran his gaze over the chiselled lettering below the middle chimney stack that the three terraced cottages had once been another pub. The gardens looked well established, and he supposed the pub had gone out of business a long time ago.

'What's the name of the pub next to the church?'

'The White Horse. That place there used to be called The Red Lion – I think it closed about eight years ago.'

'So, this publican we're about to interview must be doing well for himself if he's the only pub in the village.'

'You'd hope so. My cousin owns a pub up in Wales and it's bloody hard work.'

Moments later, Jan slowed the vehicle and steered it into the gravel-strewn car park to the White Horse.

Turpin climbed from the car and stretched his back, casting his eyes over the building in front of him.

The pub appeared to have been extended over the years, its thatched roof stretching across both the original footprint and that of a newer looking extension. Two tall chimneys poked through the layers of combed wheat reed, and a television satellite dish had been fixed to the side of one chimney, its white disc jarring against the more traditional brickwork.

Behind him, a crow called from its roost in the churchyard before its mournful cry was drowned out by the engine of a car passing by.

Blackberry blossom covered the brambles that climbed the stone wall between the properties, a promise of fruit laden with flavour only months away.

The whole atmosphere conspired against the chilling scene he'd witnessed at the church only a few hours ago, and an involuntary shiver crossed his shoulders.

'Is this freehold or leasehold?' he said as she pocketed the car keys and joined him.

'Leasehold. The current owner has been here for three years – I took a look at the initial statements that have been gathered so far, and it sounds like Terry Benedict has turned the place around since he's been here. I did an Internet search on the place this morning, and the pub company nearly closed it down before he took over because it was losing money hand over fist. The locals were up in arms.'

'He's well respected, then?'

'Seems so, yes. Doesn't suffer fools, either. One of the regulars told uniform that when Terry first arrived, he banned six people in the first week for unruly behaviour and drunkenness.'

'He must serve a good beer to keep this place going.'

'He's won a few awards, according to the *Good Pub Guide*. I get the impression that's how he got rid of the youngsters – he stopped serving what they like to drink, and so everybody else came back.'

'I can't wait to meet him.'

He led the way across the car park, then held open the door into the pub for Jan.

As his eyes adjusted to the gloom, he heard the low sound of a blues guitar playing through speakers set into the ceiling, the three-chord sequence interrupted on a regular basis by the sound of glasses clinking together from the direction of the bar.

Above his head, dark exposed beams broke up a plain white ceiling, while his shoes echoed on a parquet flooring that showed signs of wear and a well-trod path to the bar.

The walls had been painted a deep russet on one side, while on the others a patterned wallpaper provided a backdrop to a number of prints and photographs depicting the village.

A figure appeared behind the bar, rising from a crouching position before taking a step back in surprise.

'Sorry – I didn't hear the door open. Just restocking the fridges.'

'Terry Benedict?' Mark held up his warrant card.

'That's me. I presume you're here about Seamus.' He shook his head, then reached across the bar for a towel and wiped his hands. 'Terrible business, that.'

'Did you know him well?'

A sad smile crossed the man's face and he pointed at a brass plaque pinned to one end of the bar. 'We used to call it "the confessional". It's where Seamus used to sit of an evening, and we always used to laugh at the fact that people would tell him anything. It was a running joke between us.'

'Did he mind?'

'I don't think so. He used to say it was an occupational hazard.'

'How long had you known each other for?'

Benedict dropped the towel back onto the bar and moved to a cash drawer that had been left beside the till, lifting it into place and turning a key on top of the register. A series of green-coloured digits flashed to life on a screen, and then he turned back to them.

'He was one of the originals who was here when I first arrived. I think every village has them – the ones who congregate at the bar of an evening or on a Sunday lunchtime. Seamus was different to the others though, in that he didn't try to tell me how to run my business,' he added, his face rueful. 'I'll miss chatting with him, to be honest.'

'You got on well with him?'

The man's mouth thinned. 'Most of the time. We had our differences over the years, of course.'

'Tell me about the car park. I understand there may have been an issue between you and Seamus about that.'

Benedict sighed, gestured to a table with four chairs, then ran a hand over his hair. 'So, now I'm a suspect, am I?'

Mark pulled out a chair for Jan, then lowered himself into one opposite the publican.

'Best I ask the questions. Well?'

Benedict leaned back in his seat and crossed his arms over his chest. 'It all came to a head last month. To be honest, he'd been nagging me on and off all year, but I think there was a particularly big wedding on the Saturday morning. We had a private party here on Friday night, and of course the car park was full. Anyway, a few of the locals chose to walk home so they could have a drink, and I think a lot of people planned to call in when the pub opened the next day to collect their keys. By then, it was already bedlam out there because half the wedding guests couldn't park at the church.'

'So, they opted to try and park at the pub instead? How does that work – it's your land, isn't it?'

'Sort of. There's an easement between the church

and the car park out there. The agreement is that the church can use the pub car park as an overspill for events – the by-law has been in place since the 1930s, and of course there weren't that many cars around then.'

'Ever investigated whether the easement could be changed?'

'No. We had always muddled along before.' He shrugged, and dropped his hands to the table. 'Seems stupid now, in hindsight.'

'Did you and Seamus argue often?'

'No, not at all. We used to bicker light-heartedly of an evening if he was in for a drink – he loved a debate, and it was always entertaining. I can't believe he's gone.'

'Can you think of anyone who would want to harm him?'

Benedict shook his head. 'I've been thinking about that all morning. It's a close-knit community here – and I realise how rare that is in this day and age. The youngsters move on as soon as they're able, usually when they go to university, but a lot of people my age have been here for a number of years now, and quite a few people retire from London and move here.'

'Back to last night. Were you behind the bar at all times?'

'No. I had Gemma and Beverley helping behind

the bar, and three in the kitchen. We were busy – people usually come in early to eat before the band kicks off their first set, and those that don't then typically order a snack in between the music. What with our usual regulars as well as people that follow the band, I spent most of the night pulling pints, changing barrels or running up and down the stairs to the office to get loose change for the till.'

'Is there anyone who can account for your movement last night?'

Benedict frowned. 'I gave a list with the kitchen staff and the girls' contact details on it to the police officer this morning. I meant what I said. I'd never hurt Seamus.'

Mark pushed his chair back and beckoned to Jan. 'We'll let you get back to work, Mr Benedict. We'll be in touch, I'm sure.'

CHAPTER NINE

Mark held open the door for Jan, then crossed the room to his desk, sinking into his seat with an ill-disguised sigh.

He picked up the new security card and mobile phone that had been left next to his keyboard, then ran a hand across tired eyes.

Despite every senior investigating officer's training that stated the first twenty-four hours of a murder enquiry were the most important, it didn't always mean a breakthrough occurred.

He reckoned he and his colleagues would be chipping away at the veneer around the picture-perfect village life portrayed within the witness statements for some time yet.

Raucous laughter from the far side of the room snapped him from his reverie, and he looked over to see

Jan placing the carrier bag full of rubbish on Alex's desk.

'I already have two kids to look after, McClellan,' she said. 'I don't need a third.'

The young detective constable had the decency to blush as he picked up the bag, and scurried away in the direction of the waste bins at the far end of the room.

Jan shook her head as she walked towards her desk and saw him looking at her. 'Honestly, if he applied the same diligence to tidying up after himself as he does to his work, it wouldn't be such a problem.'

Mark grinned, and then his stomach rumbled – a reminder that he hadn't eaten anything since Jan had given him a sandwich earlier that morning. Since then, he'd survived on coffee, tea, and adrenalin.

He eyed up the packet of chocolate biscuits that she had placed next to her computer monitor, then discarded the thought.

He had put on weight too easily in the months spent recovering from his injuries sustained in an incident in Wiltshire, and it had taken all of his resolve to get his fitness levels back to normal.

Instead, he turned his attention to his notes from the first day's work and began to update the HOLMES2 database, the sound of Jan's fingers tapping at the keyboard of her own computer.

He didn't mind the administrative side of his role.

He found that the work enabled him to review conversations in his mind, his recollection of words and body language often raising new avenues of enquiry. Often, it was what wasn't said by witnesses that provided the breakthrough.

People forgot how expressive their eyes, hands and facial expressions could be.

Jan peered around her computer monitor. 'You don't think Terry Benedict is our killer, then?'

'It's only gut feel. We can't rule him out completely at this point.'

She returned to her work.

A moment later, he could feel eyes upon him once more and lifted his gaze. 'What?'

'Most people around here would've nicked a biscuit by now.'

'Don't tempt me. I was trying to be good.'

Her laughter was cut short by DI Kennedy hurrying into the incident room.

'Right, briefing, everyone. Now. I've got a meeting to go to in thirty minutes, so let's get this done.'

He signalled to the team to join him by the whiteboard and paced the carpet while he waited for the assembled detectives and uniformed officers to settle, then pivoted on his toes to face them. 'Have all the witness statements come in?'

'They've all been received, guv, but they won't all be updated to HOLMES2 until the morning,' said a uniformed officer close to where the DI stood. 'We've been promised some extra administrative help, but no word on when they're going to turn up.'

Kennedy acknowledged the murmured grumbles that filled the room, then held up his hand for silence. 'We knew it would happen. Peter, do what you can with what you've got. Prioritise the statements taken from people that live closest to the church.'

The uniformed officer nodded, then lowered his gaze and wrote in his notebook.

The DI turned his attention to Mark. 'How did you two get on?'

'We spoke to Helen Wilson, the church sacristan. Apart from taking us through the events of this morning, she mentioned that our priest had what she called "an altercation" with the pub landlord last month about the car parking. After that, we went and spoke to Terry Benedict, the landlord. He assured us it was an ongoing minor dispute and that they did no more than bicker about it. The details of the kitchen and bar staff were given to uniform, so Jan and I will go through the statements and correlate those with Benedict's to make sure there are no gaps.'

The DI updated the whiteboard with Mark's

comments and recapped the pen. 'Let me know if you find anything that gives you cause for concern. McClellan – how are those statements coming along?'

The young DC rose from his chair, notebook in shaking hand. 'Guv, me and Caroline have been working through the ones from the house-to-house enquiries, and we've traced Seamus's movements in the twenty-four hours leading up to his death. We haven't found anything to raise concerns. I've also put in requests for his phone records and bank statements.'

'Good man.' Kennedy waved the detective back to his seat, and then progressed around the room, seeking updates from each of the investigative team, delegating tasks and providing encouragement where necessary before bringing the briefing to a close.

'All right, that's it for today. I want you all back here at seven-thirty tomorrow morning.'

The group began to disperse, and Mark flicked his jacket off the back of his chair and began to move towards the door.

He held it open for Jan and then walked with her to the car park.

'Do you want a lift?' she said.

He peered up at the sky for a moment. 'No, thanks anyway. It's a nice evening and I need to pick up something to eat on the way home. See you in the morning, yeah?'

'Will do.' She threw a wave over her shoulder as she turned towards her car.

Mark walked along the pathway at the side of the building until he reached the main road.

The push and shove of the passing traffic became white noise to his ears as he walked.

He mulled over his first day. A major crimes unit could be stressful at the best of times but, despite his initial reservations, his new colleagues seemed to be a tight-knit team. No-one had asked too many questions, no-one had pried into his joining the team too closely, and he'd survived the encounter with Gillian.

His stomach rumbled, and he picked up his pace.

Ten minutes later, he pushed through the door of a fish and chip shop he'd discovered when he first arrived in town, and the aroma of batter, salt and vinegar teased his senses.

Two teenage girls managed the front of desk operation of the business, taking orders, handing out change, and distributing the parcels of food. Peering over the shoulder of the woman in front of him, Mark could see through a door to where a woman and two men worked in the kitchen, the clatter of metal cooking trays on steel countertops and the hiss of frying oil reaching his ears.

Almost salivating, he tapped his foot while he

waited in the short queue, and then placed his order. Cod and chips for one – plus a sausage for Hamish.

The fish and chip shop provided tables and chairs for customers while they waited for their orders, but seeing that they'd all been taken, Mark stood to one side and leaned against a tall refrigerator containing soft drinks.

He turned his attention to a television set on a wall bracket above the tables as the evening news began, tuning out the hustle and bustle around him.

The opening sequence for the programme ended, and a male newscaster faced the camera, at which point Mark realised the sound had been muted.

Undeterred, he continued to watch the flickering images, and then straightened at the sight of a "breaking news" banner that flashed across the screen. The image of the studio changed to one of a female reporter standing in a narrow lane.

Behind her, Mark recognised the low wall of the churchyard at Upper Benham. As the reporter continued to talk, the image changed to show the crime scene tape fluttering between two gate posts set into the wall while forensic investigators moved back and forth, their heads bowed as they worked in the fading light.

He checked his watch, and realised that the DI

wouldn't have seen the news report due to the meeting he said he'd been summoned to attend after the briefing. He cursed under his breath, wondering what impact the television coverage would have on the phone lines that night.

'You all right?'

He turned to find the girl behind the counter staring at him, and forced a smile. 'Yes.'

She held up a wrapped bundle. 'Here you go.'

'Thanks.'

He took the fish and chips from her and pushed his way out of the shop, sidestepping to avoid a pedestrian coming the other way, and turned right into Bridge Street.

At his back, a peal of bells began to ring out from the church of St Nicholas, and for the first time he realised how melancholy the effect was.

When he reached the boat, Hamish was sitting on the towpath, his tail a blur of movement.

The dog rose to his feet and bounded towards him, and Mark smiled as some of the stress from the day eased.

'It didn't take you long to suss out the routine,' he said, and bent down to scratch the dog between its ears. 'Come on – let's eat.'

Twenty minutes later, he sat on the roof of the

narrowboat, idly picking at the leftover chips and occasionally tossing one down onto the deck for Hamish. The dog had dispatched the sausage in less than thirty seconds, despite Mark feeding him a little at a time for fear of giving him indigestion.

Now they sat in companionable silence as the last peal of the bells receded in the distance.

The final toll flattened the buoyancy of his mood, and he quickly sobered at the thought of the body of the priest languishing in the morgue in Oxford.

The wind turned, nipping at his neck from the watercourse behind him. He uncurled his legs with a stifled groan as he eased out the kinks in his muscles. Scrunching up the empty chip papers and placing them in a dustbin at the far end of the deck, he made sure Hamish had settled onto the old duvet that served as his bed and turned to go inside.

Movement caught his eye, a figure moving around inside the narrowboat next door, her petite frame silhouetted against the light.

Lucy O'Brien had welcomed him to his temporary waterside home three weeks ago with a four-pack of lager and a homemade lasagne.

Describing herself as a budding artist – something he discovered later as being a significant understatement – she had spent the evening regaling him with stories about his other neighbours and their foibles.

He hadn't laughed so hard in months.

Now, he wondered if he should venture over. Perhaps he could take a bottle of wine.

The light went out, and he sighed.

Maybe another night, then.

CHAPTER TEN

The next morning, Mark stifled a yawn and ran his eyes over the notices that had been pinned to a corkboard next to the till in the coffee shop.

Early May, and it seemed every community group in the area was having a fête or other fundraising event over the coming weeks.

The clatter and roar from the barista's machine muted the conversation around him while the aroma of roasting beans filled the air, and a steady stream of customers pushed through the door from the street as they collected their orders on the way to work.

Warmth from the croissant in the paper bag in his hand tingled his fingertips, and his stomach rumbled.

'Flat white for Mark?'

He stepped forward to the counter, thanked the young girl who managed the till and waited on the few tables in the café with effortless grace, and then stepped out onto the busy pavement.

The early morning held a freshness to the air, the opposite side of the street bathed in a weak sunlight while the path where he walked remained in shadow. He quickened his pace, darted between the nose-to-tail traffic, and crossed the road.

His thoughts returned to his first day. Being roused from his slumber by a grumpy detective constable hadn't factored into his plans when he had moved to the Vale of the White Horse. He had fully intended to ease himself back into work after his sabbatical, and the priest's murder had been an unpleasant welcome to his new surroundings.

Of course, he'd worked on plenty of murder enquiries in the past – it was his experience that had caught the attention of Thames Valley Police when he had applied for the transfer. The sheer brutality of Carter's death worried him, though.

A shiver crawled over his shoulders, despite the sunlight.

It was as if the killer had saved all his rage for the church minister.

But why?

He paused, placed his take-out coffee cup on a low wall outside a dentist's surgery, and unwrapped the croissant.

The light texture and buttery flavour hit all his senses as he took the first mouthful, and he screwed up the paper bag before shoving it in his coat pocket. He took a tentative sip of the coffee, winced as the hot liquid burnt his tongue, and then set off once more.

He savoured the opportunity to take in his surroundings – in Wiltshire, he had lived several miles from the police station to which he had been posted and had to commute by car at the start and end of each shift. The close proximity of the rental boat's mooring to Abingdon police headquarters was something that had piqued his interest when he'd seen it advertised.

The compact nature of the market town's centre saved him the trouble of acquiring a car of his own for the time being as well, especially as Debbie was now using his old one to ferry the girls back and forth from school so they no longer had to walk. With any luck, he could get by using pool cars – especially as Jan seemed content to be designated driver.

He finished the last of the croissant and licked his fingers.

Two mini roundabouts loomed ahead, traffic slowing to a crawl as it approached the busy junction. He took the opportunity to navigate the street by way of a pedestrian crossing, and picked up his pace as the police headquarters came into view.

Moments later, he pushed through the front door

into the reception area, then paused at the sound of raised voices.

The sergeant at the front desk, whose name escaped Mark, held up his hands as he tried to placate a tall man standing in front of him.

The man was having none of it – he paced in front of the desk, pointing a finger at the sergeant while berating him.

'This is outrageous. I insist on seeing the detective in charge of this investigation immediately.'

'I'm sorry, sir. As I've already explained, Detective Inspector Kennedy isn't available at the moment. If you would care to make an appointment, I can check his diary with him later this morning and arrange a mutually convenient time for you to speak with him.'

'Don't be ridiculous. One of my constituents has been murdered, and I expect to be brought up to date with the enquiry.'

The beleaguered sergeant caught sight of Mark, and visibly relaxed as he approached the desk.

'Perhaps I can be of assistance, Mr—'

The man spun on his heel, then took a step back in surprise at the close proximity of Mark. His brow creased, further deepening his already pinched features.

'Gerald Aitchison. And you are?'

'Detective Sergeant Mark Turpin. I work with Detective Kennedy.'

'Turpin, eh? Strange name for an officer of the law.'

Mark raised an eyebrow.

'I'm the local councillor for Upper Benham.' The man's chest expanded, and he straightened his shoulders. 'I knew Seamus well. As you can understand, our local residents are extremely concerned about his murder, and are seeking reassurances that the police are doing everything in their power to apprehend the person responsible.'

Mark glanced over his shoulder at the sound of the main doors opening once more, took one look at the elderly couple that entered, and turned back to Aitchison.

'Why don't you come through here? There's a meeting room we can use, and I can bring you up to date.'

Aitchison's mouth downturned as if he had been expecting him to put up more of a fight.

Mark ignored the look of relief that the sergeant shot him, swiped his pass card and pushed open the door for Aitchison. 'Second door on the left.'

Thankfully, the lower-floor interview rooms were quiet, and as he hit the light switches he gestured to Aitchison to take a seat.

Aitchison lowered his bulk into one of the plastic

chairs, and clasped his hands on the table in front of him.

Mark pulled out a chair opposite, leaned back and tugged at his tie.

'So, what can you tell me?' said Aitchison, his face eager.

'Absolutely nothing,' said Mark. 'We're a little over twenty-four hours into our investigation. As you will appreciate, we have a number of local people to interview, witness statements to collate, and forensic evidence that needs to be reviewed and acted upon.'

Confusion spread across the other man's face, and he sat back in his seat. 'But I thought you wanted to talk to me?'

'You said you wanted reassurance that we're doing everything in our power to find the person responsible for Seamus Carter's death. I am giving you that reassurance.'

Aitchison's eyes narrowed. 'You're new here, aren't you?'

'That's right. Transferred from Wiltshire.'

'Right, Mr—'

'Detective Sergeant Turpin.'

'Well, I have to say I'm disappointed with your attitude. I thought—'

'You thought I was going to give you information about an ongoing investigation before we've even had a chance to develop a media strategy. In cases like this, everything we do has to be carefully coordinated. The first twenty-four hours of any investigation are the most important, and we cannot afford to be distracted in our work by members of the public demanding an update at every turn.'

Aitchison's mouth opened and shut, then his cheeks turned red.

Mark held up his hand. 'Be very careful with what you're about to say. I understand that you're frustrated, but that won't change our stance, and I can further assure you my senior investigating officer will support me in that.'

The councillor's shoulders heaved, and he seemed to wrestle with his anger before he emitted a loud sigh.

'You're right, of course. I'm sorry. Seamus was well liked and respected within our community. It's been such a shock.'

Mark softened his tone. 'I understand. I would imagine a lot of the locals are turning to you in their time of need, would that be correct?'

Aitchison straightened. 'It's what I'm best at. Community relations. Pulling everyone together.'

'Then that's what you need to do. Go back to your constituents, tell them the police enquiry is in its early stages but that we're doing everything possible to find Seamus's killer. But, let us do our job. As soon we have anything we can tell the public, we'll do so by way of a coordinated media release.'

The man cleared his throat, and pushed his chair back. 'If you do have any more information that you can let me have, will you call me? Especially if it might affect my constituents. We are very close-knit.'

Mark took the card Aitchison held out. 'I'll do what I can.'

Aitchison nodded, and then followed him back out to the reception area before pushing his way through the main doors and out to the car park.

'Thanks, Sarge,' said the officer behind the desk, relief in his eyes. 'He can be a pain in the arse at the best of times.'

'I got that impression,' said Mark.

CHAPTER ELEVEN

Jan glanced up from her computer as the door to the incident room opened and Turpin hurried to his desk.

'Everything all right?'

He threw his jacket over the back of his chair. 'I had the pleasure of bumping into one of your local councillors downstairs – Aitchison.'

'Lucky you.' She smirked, throwing down her pen and leaning back in her seat. 'What did he have to say for himself?'

'He was trying to stick his nose in to find out where we were up to with the murder enquiry. Obviously has no idea how a police investigation works.'

'He's a pain in the arse.'

He grinned. 'That seems to be the general consensus around here.'

'Gerald Aitchison. Local member for Ditmarsh –

including Upper Benham – apparently has sights on a minor Cabinet position.'

'Ambitious type, then.'

'Yes, be careful. Rumour has it he has the ear of the Police Commissioner.'

'Point taken.'

She straightened in her seat as the DI appeared at the door and strode towards the whiteboard, clicking his fingers to get everyone's attention.

'Come on, everyone. Enough gossip. We've got plenty to do this morning.'

He waited until they had all scurried closer, pulling up chairs or perching on desks, then turned his attention to a sheaf of paperwork in his hand. 'All right. First point to kick us off – I met with DCI Melrose and Sarah from the media relations team late yesterday, and a statement will be released at nine o'clock this morning to assure the public of our current status. Obviously, yesterday's sensationalist reporting by the press hasn't helped us, but we've been allocated two additional officers to assist with phone calls, although only the Crimestoppers number has been included within the statement for the public.' He shrugged. 'You know what it can be like though – I'm sure we'll get some calls through here, including from the usual time wasters.'

He waited for the chorus of groans to subside.

'Right, progress report. We have the preliminary pathology findings from Gillian Appleworth. She'll be conducting the post mortem first thing tomorrow morning, but for now has confirmed cause of death was the priest's throat being slit after his tongue was removed. Jan – I'd like you to attend the post mortem, please. Take Mark with you. He may as well find out where our esteemed pathologist has her lair.'

Jan glanced over to where Turpin leaned against the wall, and noticed his brow furrow at the suggestion. She stifled a groan – post mortems weren't pleasant to attend at the best of times, and now she would have to deal with the antagonism between her new sergeant and his ex-wife's sister.

The DI continued, oblivious to both Jan and Turpin's reticence.

'This morning's tasks. McClellan – work with Caroline to pull together background checks and employment history for Seamus Carter. We know he's been in Upper Benham for fifteen years, and wouldn't hurt a fly, but we also know in cases like this it's often someone the victim knows. Flag anything that warrants further investigation, and let me have a note of that an hour before this afternoon's briefing. That way, if we need to pursue something, we can set tasks for tomorrow morning and keep this investigation moving forward.'

Jan peered at the smartly dressed woman who hovered next to McClellan's desk.

DC Caroline Roberts had joined the local policing area two years ago from Hampshire, and had already proved to be an asset to the major crimes team on a previous case. Tall, slender, her blonde hair gathered up into a tidy bun at the nape of her neck, she exuded confidence.

Jan relaxed a little. Caroline was more than capable of working with Alex to manage the background checks and identify any issues that might have a bearing on the investigation.

'Mark and Jan – I've been reviewing the witness statements taken by uniform. There's a Penny Starling I'm interested in. Runs the local florist and also provides the flower arrangements for the church. She said she employs another woman, Candice Williams, but she wasn't around when uniform tried to speak with her. Only works part-time apparently, so we need to track her down. She hasn't returned the call uniform left for her. Can you two follow up with the pair of them today? See if they can shed any light on this. Someone in that village knows something, and I'm not convinced yet about Terry Benedict's assertions that his argument with Carter amounted to nothing.'

'Guv,' said Jan, and scribbled a note to herself.

The briefing concluded soon after that, and she

wheeled her chair back to her desk as Mark approached.

'I was thinking,' he said. 'Given what the guv was saying about not ruling anyone out at the moment, do you fancy having another drive around the village? I wouldn't mind getting my bearings to find out where some of these people who provided witness statements live in proximity to the church.'

She leaned across her desk to pick up her mobile phone, slipped it into her bag and pulled her jacket off the back of her chair. 'Sounds good to me – let's go.'

Before they could reach the door, however, DI Kennedy stuck his head out of his office door and called them over.

'Guv?' said Mark.

'Tom Wilcox on the desk downstairs said you spoke to Gerald Aitchison this morning. What did he want?'

'He was asking about the progress of the investigation.'

'I forgot his constituency included Upper Benham.' The DI ran his hand over his jaw. 'What did you say to him?'

'I suggested he keep an eye out for our media releases. He seemed okay about it – certainly walked out of here calmer than he was when I got here this morning.'

Kennedy's mouth thinned. 'Good, well done. Let me know if he causes either of you any ongoing issues.'

'Will do, guv. I've got one of his business cards, and if there is something we can let him know – and perhaps if he learns new information that in turn will help our investigation, he should speak to you first.'

'Appreciated. Something that you may have missed, given that you've only arrived here recently, is that there's a by-election coming up, and he intends to win it.'

NONE THE WISER

CHAPTER TWELVE

Jan managed to find a parking space next to Upper Benham's village green, a sumptuous grassed area that bordered the duck pond.

In the distance, an older man steered a ride-on lawnmower between two white wooden screens, the whirr of the motor reaching her as she opened her door and put on her sunglasses.

Turpin shrugged off his jacket, and after noticing the state of the back seat of the pool car, elected to drape it over the headrest instead and shut the door.

'Idyllic place. I mean, I suppose it is, usually.' He jerked his thumb at a sign next to the green, proclaiming "Oxfordshire's Tidiest Village 2015".

'Proud, too,' said Jan. 'Did you notice the post office we passed on the way in?'

'Yes – I saw on the system this morning that

uniform had already spoken to the woman who runs it. I was surprised how much trade they do for such a small village.'

'I get the impression there are a few enterprising people who live around here. Businesses run from home, that sort of thing, so it probably keeps them going. Did any of the statements make a note of who was responsible for the upkeep of the green? I mean, look at that grass – I'd be scared to let my boys go anywhere near it.'

'That? You're looking at a classic village cricket green. I'm sure it gets churned up every Saturday morning in the summer.' He dropped his hand and turned when he stood. 'Right, where shall we start?'

Jan pointed across the pond. 'The church is over there, and the crime scene investigators haven't come back to us with any evidence from the path between the pub and the church, so I suppose Seamus's attacker may have walked down the lane towards the green here. Of course, that's if he walked, and didn't use a car.'

'Okay, well, until we get information back about ANPR data and CCTV from cameras on the main roads around here, let's keep an open mind. Let's start with the florist's shop.'

Jan followed him across the freshly mown grass, a sense of guilt tweaking her senses as her shoes sank into the soft turf. She could imagine that on a normal summer's day, the green would host a village fête with traditional games, and plenty of laughter.

Now, the centre of the village appeared desolate, in shock at the events of the past few days.

Typical of many English villages, the centre was bisected by a main road. Although it was not a main thoroughfare, cars eased past the parked vehicles on each side of the street, and Jan realised that none of the properties bordering the green had garages. It seemed that even owners of premium-priced properties had to park on the road, and she winced as a battered four-wheel drive came perilously close to clipping the door mirror of a luxury sports car she knew for a fact would have cost the owner upwards of eighty thousand pounds.

Turpin chuckled at her sharp intake of breath. 'Don't worry. I'm sure they're insured.'

'They'd need to be.'

The florist's shop took up the corner of a row of terraced houses, next to a hairdressing salon. Both properties had been converted at some point to house the businesses, and as Jan craned her neck upwards, she realised the upper floor of each remained as residential use, given the patterned curtains that hung in the windows.

Dark-green signage with gold lettering framed the

front door, whilst colourful buckets of ready-made bouquets boarded the pavement and threshold.

Jan noticed ruefully that the colours were funereal in nature.

'Every cloud...' she muttered as Turpin followed her through the open door.

An electronic two-tone *beep* from an alarm above the door sounded somewhere behind the counter, and a disembodied voice called from a room out the back.

'Be there in a sec!'

A muffled curse followed, and then the sound of rushing water before a red-faced woman appeared, her blotchy complexion stark against dark-grey hair.

'Oh,' she said as Jan held up her warrant card. She dried her hands on her apron, then pushed a tendril of hair behind her ear. 'Sorry. Late delivery of agapanthus. Penny will kill me if I don't get them watered properly.'

'Are you Candice Williams?'

'That's right.'

'We've been expecting a phone call from you,' said Jan. 'Our colleagues left a message for you on Sunday. Why haven't you been in touch?'

Candice threw up her hands. 'I knew there was something I was meant to do. I'm so sorry – I listened to the message, then deleted it but forgot to write it down. Penny is always telling me I'd forget my own head if it wasn't screwed on.'

She chuckled, but Jan said nothing and Turpin remained stony-faced.

'Anyway,' said Candice, her smile fading, 'I suppose you'll be wanting to ask me about Father Carter, right?'

'Where were you on Saturday between ten o'clock Saturday night and seven o'clock Sunday morning?' said Jan.

'Well, I got home from shopping on Saturday – in Abingdon, mind. It was the big shop. Ran out of everything by Thursday, I had. So, I got in about six o'clock, I suppose. Of course, by then Marbles was going spare for his supper—'

'Marbles?' said Turpin.

'My cat. Twenty-one years. Doesn't look a day over eight, mind. You should see his—'

'Saturday night, Mrs Williams?' said Jan.

'It's Ms. Yes. Saturday. So – once his lordship had been fed, then it was time for my tea and I plonked myself in front of the telly for the rest of the evening.'

'What was on?'

'Oh, that escape overseas thing to start with. Australia, it was. Very nice. Don't know if I could live in a city like Sydney though. Country girl myself...' She caught Turpin's glare and cleared her throat. 'Um, and then I watched a film until about nine or so. One of them spy things. Love some action and adventure, me.'

Jan bit her lip hard to stop the smile that was threatening, and avoided meeting her colleague's gaze.

'What about the hours of nine o'clock and seven o'clock the next morning?' she said.

'Oh, that was me out for the count,' said Candice. She lowered her voice and smiled. 'Treated myself to a couple of glasses of sherry, you see. I don't drink much, so that did for me. I didn't wake up until Penny phoned me with the news Helen had found Father Carter.' She shuddered. 'Terrible. Truly shocking, that.'

'How long have you worked here?' said Turpin.

'It feels like ages, but it's only been four years. Penny's a brilliant boss.' Candice beamed, and pointed at a framed newspaper article next to the till that showed a slim blonde-haired woman being presented with a certificate by a broad man wearing mayoral chains around his shoulders. 'She even won a local business venture prize a couple of years ago, look.'

'Do you provide flowers for the church on a regular basis?' said Jan.

'When they need them, yes,' said Candice. 'Most weeks they make do with what people donate from their gardens this time of year – Penny still goes along to oversee the flower arranging, mind.'

Jan flipped her notebook shut. 'Do you know where we might find Penny?'

'She went out about twenty minutes ago.' Candice glanced over her shoulder. 'I really do need to sort out the agapanthus, if you don't need me for anything else.'

'Thanks, Ms Williams.'

Jan followed Turpin out of the shop and rolled her eyes at him as he paused on the pavement, an ill-disguised smile on his face.

'Good grief,' she said. 'That was like speaking with my mother. How on earth has Penny Starling managed to work with someone like that for four years? As for the bloody cat – Marbles?'

'I think Ms Williams has lost hers.'

Jan laughed. 'You could be right. What do you want to do next?'

'Let's take another look at the church.'

CHAPTER THIRTEEN

Turpin checked for oncoming traffic, and then gestured to Jan to follow him across the road before he paused on the kerb at the junction with the lane from the church.

She pushed her sunglasses up onto her head and moved across the road to the opposite side, her head bowed as she scanned the asphalt.

'No sign of skid marks,' she called.

'I didn't think there would be. I think if our killer had a car and left the village this way, he'd have been driving carefully so as not to draw attention to himself.'

Jan conceded the point, and began to walk away from the green towards the church.

She kept her eyes on the gutter, scanning for any items that might have been jettisoned by a passing car, and then stepped out of the way as a red post office van eased to a standstill at the gate to an ivy-covered cottage behind her.

As she drew opposite the entrance to the church car park, she sighed and crossed the road once more to join Turpin who was crouching next to a drain.

'The only problem with being a tidy village is that there's no bloody evidence left, Sarge.'

He straightened and brushed off his trousers as she approached. 'Well, the CSIs didn't find anything either so I guess it was a long shot.'

'Or our killer was simply careful.'

He turned and peered over the stone wall bordering the church, his ample height giving him a clear view across to the front door. 'Did you hear if the CSIs had finished with the church?'

'Late yesterday, according to Caroline.'

'Let's head over there. I want to take another look at where Seamus was found.'

'Okay.'

A breeze caught her hair as they approached the nineteenth-century building, and she pulled out a hair elastic from her bag, expertly twisting it at the nape of her neck as she took in the surrounding landscaped grounds.

'It's unusual to have a church like this in a village,' she said.

'What do you mean?'

'Well, after the Reformation, any land remaining was eventually built on – usually with materials from the destroyed Catholic churches, so it's rare that you find one in the centre of a community like Upper Benham. I looked up the history of this place last night. Apparently, back in the 1800s, this parcel of land belonged to a rich widow who bequeathed it to the church.'

'Blimey, I'll bet her kids were impressed. What about their inheritance, I wonder?'

She smiled. 'No kids.'

'No churchyard here.'

'Blame the nineteenth-century burial acts that came into force. I would imagine a lot of parishioners who've passed away over the years since are buried in cemeteries like the one at Garford.'

They stood for a moment, craning their necks to peer up at the intricate stonework of the building, and then Turpin tapped her on the arm.

'Come on.'

Jan raised an eyebrow as he pushed against the left-hand double door, surprised that it wasn't locked.

As they stepped over the threshold, she heard the faint sound of sobbing and as her eyes adjusted to the gloom within, she noticed a figure in one of the pews nearest the altar, head bowed.

She left Turpin where he stood and approached

the woman, who raised her head at the sound of footsteps on the flagstones.

Her eyes opened wide at the sight of Jan's warrant card.

'You're the police?'

'Yes. And you are...?'

'Penny Starling. I'm the—'

'Florist, aren't you? We were just talking with Candice. What are you doing here?'

The woman sniffed, then dabbed at her eyes with an already sodden paper tissue. 'I have a set of keys. The tape was taken down yesterday, so I thought it would be okay.'

Jan slid into the pew next to her. 'I'm Detective Constable Jan West. Why did you come here?'

Penny shrugged, her eyes bloodshot beneath a long blonde fringe. 'I didn't sleep well last night, thinking of Seamus. I thought if I came here, I'd find peace.' Her mouth twisted. 'No chance of that now. I got a phone call from the bishop's office this morning. Helen's too distraught – I don't think she'll ever come back. They're going to bring in professional cleaners. There was too much blood. She couldn't... can't face it. They—'

Another sob wracked her shoulders, and she brought her hand to her mouth to stifle the wail.

'Penny, I realise that you're devastated at what's

happened, but I'm going to have to ask for those keys. I'm sure the diocese would prefer that we keep the place secure for the time being, don't you think?'

Penny nodded.

'Is this the only set you have?' said Jan, pocketing the set of three keys that were handed over.

'Yes. I don't often use them as Seamus is – was – usually already here when I arrived. Helen had another set, but she gave them to the police when they turned up yesterday morning.'

'Do you have any family close by?'

'No. I spoke to my sister after I heard from the bishop this morning. She offered to come and stay with me, but I'd rather she didn't. We don't get on that well, and she's probably fishing for gossip, to be honest.'

Jan noted the bitter tone of the woman's voice, and glanced over her shoulder at a cough from Turpin.

'Come on,' she said. 'I'll walk you to the door, shall I?'

They slipped from the pew and made their way to the double doors, the detective sergeant holding one open for Penny.

When she drew near him, she stopped.

'When – when will his body be released? A lot of the villagers are asking. They want to pay their respects.'

'It may be a while. It depends on our investigation and the outcome of the post mortem.'

'You'll find who did this, won't you?'

'We'll do everything we can,' he said.

'Okay. 'Bye.'

Jan watched as the woman negotiated the short path to the road then turned right towards the village. She exhaled and handed the keys to Turpin.

'Thanks.' He checked his watch. 'We've got forty minutes until the briefing.'

Jan followed him through the church to the parish rooms at the rear where Carter's body had been discovered.

A ferrous smell remained in the musty air, and as he pushed open the door to the priest's office, she understood why.

Stains covered the thin carpet and walls where Carter's blood had congealed and dried.

Jan reared backwards as a bluebottle fly buzzed close to her face, and then placed her hand over her mouth and nose.

Turpin wore an expression she was sure she hid under her fingers.

'Uniform gave the church a note of a professional cleaning service, didn't they?' he said, his nose wrinkling as his gaze swept the room.

'That's what Penny said. I guess if the place only

got released by the CSIs late yesterday though, they might not be able to schedule it in for a few days.'

'Bloody hell. Just as well you got those keys off of Penny.'

He hovered at the threshold, as if he were unwilling to progress further into the room, and Jan moved past him so she could peer closer at the desk.

'Why on earth kill him here?' she said.

'Rather than at home, you mean?'

'Yeah. I mean, hell of a risk, wasn't it? Anyone could've walked in on the killer.'

'Not if Seamus had the place locked and the killer waited until he felt it was safe to reveal himself.'

Jan glanced down, not wanting to step on the blood stains, and crossed to the other side of the room. She paused when she drew closer to the abandoned chair and turned back to face Turpin.

'Interesting turn of phrase.'

'What?'

'You said "reveal himself". I wonder if he did? I wonder if the killer showed his face to Seamus?'

'Well, Gillian said he was attacked from behind, so the rope was thrown over his head before it was jerked backwards to expose his throat.'

'But it'd be hard to remove someone's tongue from that angle, wouldn't it? Easier to secure the rope and then move around here to do that.'

He ran a hand over his jaw. 'True.'

'Maybe his killer wanted him to see his face.'

She cast a final glance over the pockmarked surface of the desk, and then at the simple crucifix on the wall above, and shook her head.

'I don't get it.'

'Me neither. There was a rage to this attack, wasn't there? Almost as if his killer had – I don't know—'

'But it was calculated up to a point, wasn't it?'

'Exactly. Even if it was premeditated, which I'm sure it was, it's like he had no control over his emotions once he was here.' His mobile phone emitted a *beep* and he jerked his eyes away from the priest's workspace at the alarm. 'We'd better get going.'

Once outside, Jan removed the elastic from her hair and slipped it over her wrist above her watch as she turned and stared up at a plaque above the door, the year of construction stamped upon it in Roman numerals. 'I wonder when the diocese will find a replacement for him? It's going to be hard for them, isn't it?'

'I know – I'll bet they won't exactly have priests lining up for the job. I mean, who on earth would want to take Seamus's place after what happened here?'

CHAPTER FOURTEEN

A warm wind rustling in the trees accompanied Mark's footsteps across the asphalt as he traipsed after Jan through the car park the next morning.

She led the way towards the double doors of the low-slung building that housed the mortuary for Oxford City Council, which also served as the site of post mortems requested by the Home Office pathologist covering the local policing area.

Jan stopped with her hand on the brass handle and turned to face him.

'What?'

'Are you going to be okay doing this, you know – with her being your ex-wife's sister and all that?'

'Of course. I'll be on my best behaviour.' He winked, but wondered if the pathologist would temper her own emotions and remain professional.

Jan forged ahead with confidence in her stride, no doubt familiar with the mortuary layout.

He wondered how often she had been asked to attend a post mortem. Despite her assurances that she had worked on murder investigations before, he wasn't convinced she had been exposed to something as brutal as Seamus Carter's slaying.

He battened down his misgivings as they approached a reception desk, behind which a lanky, acne-ridden man in his late twenties battled with an ancient computer.

'Morning, Clive,' said Jan. 'We're here for the priest's post mortem.'

The man smiled, exposing uneven teeth. 'Hi, Jan. Haven't seen you for ages.'

'Don't take this the wrong way, but I'm kind of glad about that.' She gestured to Mark. 'This is DS Mark Turpin. He's just joined us from Wiltshire.'

'And more's the pity he didn't stay there.'

Mark spun around at the sound of Gillian's voice. Despite the tension between them, he had to admit that Gillian Appleworth carried a certain presence about her as she strode towards them.

Now devoid of the baggy protective clothing she had been wearing at the crime scene, her charcoal-grey trouser suit matched the coolness of her eyes and was only softened by the pastel pink shirt she wore.

Her tone, however, was one of pure ice.

She turned to Jan. 'What did you do to deserve him?'

The detective constable's mouth dropped open, but to her credit she remained silent.

Mark forced a smile and held up his hands. 'Come on, Gillian. Can't you be civil just once – if not for me, then for the sake of these two?'

She glared back. 'Go and get suited up, the pair of you. I'll begin the post mortem in fifteen minutes. Don't be late.'

She turned on her heel and stalked away, not bothering to check if they were following as she shrugged her own protective coveralls over her shoulders.

Clive turned to him, his eyebrow raised. 'Ah, I remember now. You're her sister's ex-husband.'

He followed Gillian, chuckling under his breath.

Mark sighed. 'Bloody great.'

———————

THE STENCH of chemicals assaulted Mark's nostrils the moment the double doors swung open into the mortuary.

The waft of antiseptic failed to do anything to

disguise the pervading smell that emanated from what was laid out on the gurney.

Both he and Jan approached the body of the priest with caution, although in Mark's case his hesitation was equally a result of the close proximity of Appleworth's figure as she circled the table, adjusting her clip-on microphone.

She raised her gaze briefly to his, and then called over her shoulder to her assistant.

'All right, Clive. Give me a hand.'

Mark stepped back as the younger man brushed past him, and the examination began. He peered across at Jan who turned away when the pathologist brandished an electric saw, but to her credit she remained passive for the remainder of the procedure.

He always felt that the process of post mortem was a final insult to someone who had died so brutally. The person who would be remembered by friends and family no longer existed – what remained was a vessel from which answers would be gleaned, reports written, and, finally, if he did his job properly and was afforded a pinch of luck, a conviction handed down by a judge.

It all seemed such a waste.

Finally it was over, and as Clive began to clear away the tools and instruments used by Gillian, she turned to the two detectives and lowered her mask.

'All right. Well, based on my examination I stand by my original observations that he was alive when his tongue was removed. His killer took his time about it, too. Has it been found?'

'His tongue?' Mark frowned and took a step forward. On the gurney, the priest's face appeared passive, calm, his eyes closed as if in slumber, despite the ragged cuts to his neck and mouth. 'You mean the killer took it?'

'Well, Seamus wasn't made to swallow it as we first thought,' she said, her eyes clouding. 'I would've found it during my examination otherwise.'

'Any idea how it was removed?' said Jan. 'I mean, what sort of weapon?'

In response, Gillian reached out and prised the priest's jaw open once more, and then took a torch and used it to illuminate the man's mouth.

'Here, take a look.'

Jan didn't hesitate, and instead joined the pathologist as she peered closer.

'See here? The cut is jagged. It's not clean. The tongue was hacked away, and given the bruising to the muscle I'd suggest the weapon had a short blade, stubby in nature. The bruising's been caused by the handle meeting the tongue each time the knife was applied. Perhaps a box cutter, or similar.'

Jan drew back, her troubled eyes meeting Mark's. 'The CSIs didn't find any discarded knives or blades when they did their search of the church.'

'Nor the churchyard or surrounding area,' he said. 'Given the amount of blood at the scene, how would our killer have transported the tongue? No signs of blood spatter were found leading away from the crime scene, were they?'

Gillian shook her head. 'Not as far as I'm aware. Could've been anything, to be honest – plastic food carton, paper kitchen towel. Anything that would contain or soak up the blood. As you say, your killer was careful and didn't leave a trail.'

For once he noted she remained professional, and he realised she was as shocked as they were by the brutal murder.

He cleared his throat as she removed her torch and returned the priest's jaw to its normal position. 'Well, we'll be getting out of your way. Thank you.'

She nodded, but remained silent as the two detectives made their way out of the room.

'I'll meet you by the front door,' said Mark as Jan moved towards the women's changing room.

'Okay.'

In the men's room, he tore the borrowed plastic coveralls from his body, placed them in a biohazard bin next to the door and stood for a moment in front of the mirrors above a row of sinks, gripping the porcelain.

Then the sweat began to pool at his forehead, and he twisted the faucet, cold water splashing over his hands before he cupped them to his face.

His thoughts returned to the destroyed body on the gurney, a harmless priest torn to pieces first for bloodlust then for medical science, and a shudder crept down his spine.

'Hold it together, Turpin,' he growled under his breath.

He snatched a handful of paper towels from the dispenser above the sink, dabbed his face dry, and then pitched the screwed-up rubbish into a wastepaper basket at his feet.

With one final glance in the mirror to check he didn't look as pale as he felt, he tore the door open and hurried into the corridor.

Jan was waiting for him by the front door, scrolling through messages on her phone, but lifted her head and smiled as he approached.

'All set?'

'Yes. Back to the station. Best we give Kennedy a quick run through prior to the briefing.'

He paused at the door, glanced over his shoulder in the direction of the mortuary, then pursed his lips and followed Jan back to the car.

'You okay, Sarge?'

'Nothing stolen from him. No hesitation in killing him. And a trophy taker.' Mark clipped his seatbelt over his chest. 'The question is, who would do that to him, Jan? And why?'

CHAPTER FIFTEEN

Jan wrinkled her nose after she took a sip of coffee before realising it had turned cold, then ran her eyes over the pages she'd retrieved from the dilapidated printer she shared with the rest of the investigation team.

Two days had passed since they'd interviewed the last of their key witnesses, and the frustrated *tap tap* of fingers on keyboards filled the incident room as the team began to sift through the information collated.

The phones had fallen silent hours ago, and a sense of desperation mixed with an already subdued atmosphere lingered in the room after the key points from the post mortem results had been shared at that morning's briefing by DI Kennedy.

A melancholy wrapped its way around Jan's

thoughts as she tried to concentrate on the lines of text in front of her.

It had taken longer to turn up than she would have liked, but she finally held in her hands a transcript sent by the diocesan office near Bristol from where Seamus Carter had transferred to Upper Benham.

Prior to becoming the priest for the village and surrounding area, he had overseen the religious duties for a parish north-west of the city for three years. Nothing untoward had been noted by the diocese at the time, and as Jan flicked through the pages and noted his prior engagement had lasted for a decade, she wondered why his stay in the parish had been so short.

To all intents and purposes, that community would have been larger than the one he administered at Upper Benham and, from reading through the witness statements, Jan felt that it was one that Carter would have thrived in.

She glanced up at movement behind her, and then Turpin placed a fresh mug of coffee at her elbow.

He took a sip from his own hot drink before gesturing to the papers in her hand.

'Any luck?'

'I'm not sure – I can't work out why Carter would have been located from a large parish like the one north of Bristol to go and work in Upper Benham.'

'It happens, I suppose. Perhaps he felt a calling to immerse himself in a smaller community.'

'Maybe, but the transfer was quick. Look – they started the paperwork in the May, and he was in Oxfordshire by July. I would have thought it would have taken longer than that because they would have had to find someone else to take his place in the parish.'

She passed the documentation to Turpin and waited while he flicked through the pages.

'I've done some digging around, and the only explanation I can come up with is that they were desperate for priests in this parish. I spoke with the bishop's administration team on Monday to get those details, and they said that most of their priests are responsible for more than one church. Take a look at the back page – you can see how large the area is that they have to cover.'

'And yet Seamus was only responsible for the parish of Upper Benham.' Mark handed back the printout. 'If it was anyone else, I'd suggest that he had a health problem and the church had put him on light duties, but we know from the post mortem that wasn't the case.'

'Maybe that was all they had on offer when they moved him?' said Kennedy as he joined them.

'Could be, I suppose,' said Turpin. 'Maybe he was

the ideal candidate for the position and he was headhunted – or the church equivalent?'

Kennedy snorted. 'Nobody's perfect. What about you, Jan? Did you glean anything useful from your conversation with the bishop's office?'

'No-one had a bad word to say about him, guv. And there's nothing to suggest there were any issues in his work to date.'

'All right. Get onto our colleagues near Bristol and ask them to follow up with Carter's old church. If our priest was so well-loved here, let's find out if someone over that way holds a grudge against him. There was a lot of hatred in this murder, so find out who he might have pissed off in his past.'

'Will do.'

'Have you found out anything more about the florist and her assistant – Penny and Candice?'

'Clean driving licences, nothing untoward on the system,' said Jan. 'Caroline cross-referenced the witness statements in HOLMES2. Helen Wilson knows them through the church, of course.'

'What did Helen have to say about them?'

'Uniform followed up with her yesterday,' said Turpin. 'She said she socialises with Penny occasionally, not so much with Candice. Not surprising, to be honest. I'd imagine Candice to be too overbearing – it was bad enough interviewing her.'

'I agree,' said Jan. 'Penny was much more reserved, even taking into consideration the shock of Seamus's murder I think she's the quieter of the two.'

'What was she doing with a set of keys to the church?' said Kennedy. 'I thought uniform accounted for all of them?'

'An oversight that's been rectified now,' said Turpin. 'I phoned the general stores in the village this morning – the owner wasn't around, but her assistant, Jim Aster, was. He confirms no additional sets of keys were cut by him in the past six months.'

'That doesn't mean our killer couldn't have obtained a copy set elsewhere,' said Kennedy. He ran a hand over his jaw as his gaze roamed the whiteboard. 'Get McClellan to phone around all locksmiths and the like within a ten-mile radius of Upper Benham.'

'Guv.'

'Have other religious leaders in the area been contacted?'

'We've had a team phoning around since Monday,' said Turpin. 'Everyone's been accounted for. We've gone with the angle that we don't think the murder is motivated by a particular religious belief, but rather a personal attack, and have recommended that people keep their doors locked when alone.'

He fell silent, and Jan noticed his shoulders sag a little.

She felt his frustration – the advice they were handing out seemed pitiful, but it was all they could do. Unless and until a motive could be established, they would be unable to do more.

'Very well,' said Kennedy. 'Then we keep going. Somewhere amongst this mess is a clue, and we need to find it – fast.'

CHAPTER SIXTEEN

Mark cursed as his thumb caught on a staple protruding from the back of the report, and glared at the offending piece of metal.

A trickle of blood began to bubble in the cut, and he fished a paper tissue from a box beside Jan's desk before collapsing back in his chair.

Running his eyes over the pages once more, he resisted the urge to sigh.

A silence permeated the incident room and, except for DI Kennedy whose office light blazed through the cracks in the blinds that afforded him privacy while he worked, the rest of the team had dispersed for the night, exhausted by the events of the week and frustrated with the lack of a lead after another twenty-four hours with little by way of a break.

Kennedy had conducted a briefing towards the end

of that afternoon, splitting up the team so that a constant presence would be maintained on the investigation over the weekend.

Mark had elected to take the Sunday off, planning to sort through the rest of his belongings that had been delivered to a storage unit at a nearby trading estate, and make a start on organising his new life.

He leaned back in his seat, his gaze falling on the early evening hues illuminating the sky beyond the windows of the incident room and wondered whether he should venture out for a pint on the way home to the boat.

He shook off the thought almost immediately.

Friday night in a town often besieged with drinkers from the nearby barracks was not his idea of fun, and chances were that he'd end up in a dingy pub on his own somewhere watching bad television in his attempts to avoid any trouble.

He checked his watch.

He'd give it another thirty minutes or so and then make a move. Anything to give him a head start in the morning – and a clear desk.

'Trying to impress the new boss?'

He spun around at the sound of the voice, its tone slicing through the calm atmosphere he'd been enjoying.

'Gillian? What're you doing here?'

The pathologist pushed Caroline's chair out of the way, its wheels catching on the plastic veneer of the mat the detective constable kept under her desk and juddering to a standstill. She ignored it, and instead advanced on him, her stride unbroken. 'He won't fall for it, you know.'

'I'm sorry, what?'

'All this. The staying late. Trying to fit in. It won't work.'

He dropped his pen, the ballpoint hitting the keyboard first before it bounced and fell to a standstill next to the box of tissues.

'You know no bounds, do you?'

'That's good, coming from you.'

'How'd you get in, anyway?'

'Tom Wilcox on the front desk gave me a guest pass and showed me up here.' Her top lip curled. 'They don't have a clue, do they?'

'Pardon?'

'About you. Why you transferred.'

'Honestly, Gillian, it's none of their business – or yours.'

She dropped her bag and the manila folder onto the desk, then leaned against it and folded her arms.

Mark scooted his chair backwards until he could lift his gaze to hers without getting a crick in his neck. 'What is it you want?'

'I want you gone.'

'What?'

'You heard me.'

'I only just got here.'

'So, transfer out again. Go back to Swindon. Sort out your marriage before it's too late.'

'Gillian, I told you – it's none of your business. I know you're worried about Debbie, but she's fine with all of this. Besides, it's better for the girls at the moment. Honest.'

She swung her hair over her shoulder. 'When was the last time you spoke to her?'

'I'm not discussing my private life with you.'

'I'd think long and hard about that transfer, Mark. It's for your own good. You're a liability to your colleagues, after all.'

He rose to his feet and jabbed his forefinger at her. 'Don't you dare threaten me.'

A faint clatter emanated from Kennedy's office.

Mark dropped his hand and checked over his shoulder as a shadow moved towards the door.

'Mark? A word of warning. If you're planning to stay, then don't mess up my life like you did my sister's.'

With that, Gillian pushed away from the desk and rose to her feet, a smile forming on her face as the door to Kennedy's office opened. 'Ewan. I'm glad I caught you here. I have my full report regarding Seamus Carter.'

'That was quick. That new intern of yours must be doing well.'

She waved her hand dismissively. 'It didn't take as long as I first thought. Quite straightforward, actually.'

'Are you on your way home?'

'Yes. I thought I'd drop this off, in case my staff haven't had a chance to email it to you yet.'

'Well, that's very good of you. Come on through. You still here, Mark?'

'About to head off, guv.'

'Very well. See you in the morning.'

Mark waited until the door closed behind the pathologist, before releasing the breath he'd been holding.

He clenched his fists, fighting down the frustration that threatened to engulf him, and then swiped his jacket off the back of his chair and stalked from the room.

CHAPTER SEVENTEEN

Mark tipped back the bottle and let the first cooling taste of beer wash some of the stress away.

He set the bottle down on the roof of the narrowboat, scratched Hamish behind the ears, and tilted his head until he could see stars breaking through the last of the cloud cover.

Summer was on the wind. He could sense it, finally.

From the direction of town, a siren wailed, and he tensed, waiting.

His mobile phone remained silent though, and as the noise faded into the distance, his shoulders began to relax.

He wouldn't admit it to anyone, but the events of the last few days had left him exhausted.

The sensation was one he resented. Before the

incident in Swindon, before the enforced sabbatical, he had prided himself on his fitness. Prior to that, he had only taken time off work when his daughters had been born. That dedication to the job was what had put paid to his marriage in time, like so many others.

'Penny for your thoughts?'

He jerked around at the voice, his heart lurching.

'Only me. Permission to board?'

Lucy stood at the gunwale, her arms wrapped around her middle as the breeze caught her dark blonde curls. She pushed her hair out of her face and smiled up at him.

'Permission granted. I thought you were leaving tonight to get to Brighton for your exhibition in the morning?'

'It's been postponed. The art space got broken into last night and vandals wrecked it.'

'Bastards. They catch anyone?'

'Yeah. Teenagers. Probably did it for a dare.'

'There's beer in the fridge.'

'Thanks.'

She disappeared from view, and moments later he heard the clink of glass. In the quiet of the riverbank, the faint hiss as she opened two bottles reached his ears and, smiling, he drained the dregs from the bottle in his hand.

Lucy reappeared, and he took one of the bottles

from her then reached out to pull her onto the roof of the narrowboat.

'Cheers,' she said, tipping her bottle against his.

They sat in companionable silence, the occasional car passing along the main road into town carrying over the night air.

After a while, Lucy placed her beer bottle on the roof and leaned back on her elbows. 'How are you settling in?'

He shrugged. 'Okay, I suppose. To be honest, I could have done with another week getting my bearings, but it doesn't always work out that way.'

'The priest's murder, you mean?'

'Yeah.'

Hamish got up from his position next to Mark and trotted to the far end of the roof to watch a pair of swans on the opposite bank, his ears alert.

Lucy chuckled. 'The neighbourhood guard dog assumes his position for the evening.'

'What do you know about him? Does anyone know who his owner is?'

'I don't think so. He just turned up one morning, although I suspect some of the older boat owners along here are familiar with him. He's certainly not starving and seems content to roam along the towpath and socialise.' She smiled. 'It's your turn now, though.'

'I think he knows a soft target when he sees one.'

'Yeah, well, you'll be popular. I don't think everyone along here wants the responsibility of keeping a lookout for him.'

'I don't mind. I used to enjoy walking my neighbours' dogs for pocket money when I was a kid. I was never allowed a dog of my own because we couldn't afford it.'

'How did you end up here, anyway?' Dimples creased her cheeks. 'That is, if I'm not being too nosy? You've never really explained.'

He drew his knees up to his chest, cradling the cold beer bottle between his hands, and then rubbed his thumb over the bubbles of condensation that clung to the glass. 'So, you're not buying the story that I was after a change of scenery when I split up with my wife?'

'Not really.' She smiled, her eyes softening in the glow from the lights on her boat. 'But you don't have to tell me if you don't want to.'

He ran a hand over the back of his neck, and then sighed.

'Circumstances beyond my control,' he said eventually. 'My wife and I broke up eight months ago. It wasn't anyone's fault – we had drifted apart, and I don't suppose the hours I was keeping with this job helped. Anyway, she met a new bloke last month—'

'That was quick.'

'I know. Bit of a shock, to be honest.'

'And you can't bear to see her with someone else.'

'Exactly.' He took a swig from the bottle.

'You have two daughters, yes? I heard from one of the neighbours along the towpath that you had visitors the other weekend while I was away.'

'Yes – Anna and Louise.'

'Got a photograph?'

Mark put down the beer bottle and reached into his wallet, his thumb tracing the girls in the image before he passed it across.

'They're pretty,' said Lucy. 'Tall, too, by the looks of it.'

'Best thing I've got to show for my thirty-eight years on the planet.'

She smiled as she handed back the photograph. 'Did they stay here with you?'

'It was just a quick visit. They're meant to stay with me every fortnight, although I've had to put them off until this investigation is solved.' He took another sip, and frowned. 'Kennedy's going to have us working all hours.'

Lucy sniffed, and straightened, twisting round to face him. 'But I'm guessing that your marriage break-up wasn't the only reason you transferred to Oxfordshire, was it?'

He narrowed his eyes. 'Are you psychic or something?'

She laughed, a pretty sound that lifted his encroaching dark mood.

'No, I'm not, but it's pretty obvious you're withholding information. You're being cagey.'

'You should have been a detective.'

She wrinkled her nose. 'I've seen the news this week. I couldn't cope with what you have to deal with on a day-to-day basis, so no thanks.'

He placed the bottle on the roof, still three quarters full. He wasn't used to talking about what had happened – not once he had left the hospital, and the police-appointed psychiatrists had signed him off for work once more.

'I'm sorry,' said Lucy. She waved her hand in front of her face as if swatting away a fly. 'I have the annoying habit of asking too many questions, and making people feel uncomfortable.'

'No, that's all right. Everyone has been skirting around the issue at work, and I've been waiting for someone to raise it there – I'm sure the rumours are swirling.'

She grinned, pulled her cardigan around her shoulders, then gave him a nudge. 'Come on, then – I don't gossip, so spill the beans.'

'Two years ago, I was called out to an incident north of Swindon. There had been a fight at a pub – the sort of place that has a reputation for that sort of thing, and they wanted a detective to attend because the person that had been stabbed was an informant of ours. He was helping with an investigation for county lines drug trafficking, and uniform weren't convinced he was going to last the night. As it turns out, they were right.'

'County lines?'

'Dealers use vulnerable kids to traffic the drugs between regions. They figure the kids are less likely to get stopped by the police.'

'That's awful. What happened?'

'While the crime scene investigation team were gathering evidence, I worked with uniform to speak with witnesses so that, if we gleaned anything from them, I could report straight back to the incident room the next morning.'

'What happened?'

'In hindsight, it was a stupid mistake.'

'Bloody hindsight.' She held up a hand. 'Sorry.'

He acknowledged the comment with a shrug. 'I know. Anyway, I got the information I needed, coordinated with uniform to get statements into the system as soon as possible the next morning, and then left the scene. I was walking back to my car when I was attacked.'

'Who by?'

'The suspect who had stabbed our informant. My car was parked on the third floor of a multi-storey. I got in the lift, and he grabbed me as the doors were closing. I wasn't wearing a vest – we'd made the mistake of assuming he had fled the scene. He still had the knife, as I found out when he stabbed me.' He swallowed and twisted the skin on his finger where the wedding band had once been. 'Fortunately for me, that didn't finish me off, and so when I collapsed on the floor he tried to throttle me.'

'Your voice...? I thought it was because you used to smoke cigarettes.'

'No – damaged larynx. They thought it might heal completely in time, but I don't believe that, to be honest. I think this is as good as it's going to get. Thank Christ two other detectives heard my shout as the doors were closing and came running. They dragged the bloke off me when the doors opened on the next floor. I was starting to pass out by then.'

Lucy hissed through her teeth and looked away from him, evidently shocked.

'Obviously I survived, but any hope of getting back together with Debbie went out the window. I think it scared her that the girls nearly lost their dad. We started to drift apart before I'd even left hospital.'

'Why the sabbatical?'

'I kept getting panic attacks – in enclosed spaces especially. Lifts, obviously, small rooms, that sort of thing.'

'But you're okay here?'

'Yeah. The windows help, you see – and I think being near the water does, too. I've found that as long as I'm somewhere well-lit, I'm all right.'

'They made you take some time off?'

He sighed. 'Yes, for the stress, apparently. It happens, I guess. I made the mistake of thinking I could cope.'

'And you bottled it all up in the hope it would all go away—' She broke off as his mobile phone began to ring.

He glanced at the number and his mouth curled. 'Sorry. Work.'

'No problem. I was about to head off anyway. Thanks for the beer.' She paused when she reached the gunwale. 'Mark? Make sure you come and find me if you need to talk, all right? No more bottling it up.'

'Thank you, I will. 'Night.' He waited until she had reached the towpath, and then hit the "answer" button. 'Mark Turpin.'

'It's Jan. There's been another one.'

CHAPTER EIGHTEEN

Jan blew on her fingers and cursed the coolness that clung to the night air, then glanced over her shoulder at the sound of a door slamming shut in time to see Turpin walking towards her, a patrol car accelerating from the kerb.

'I forgot you didn't have transport yet.'

'Don't worry. Sorry it took me so long to get here. I don't usually scrounge lifts off uniform, but they were passing.'

'I'd never suggest otherwise.'

He handed her an aluminium travel cup. 'Made you a coffee while I was waiting for them.'

'You're a star, thanks.' She twisted the lid and took a sip as his eyes scanned the terraced cottage.

'Not a church this time, then?'

'His home. The neighbour heard a commotion and

tried to rouse the priest by knocking on the front door. He became concerned when there was no answer, and called triple nine.'

'What happened?'

Jan pointed the coffee cup at the front door. 'When uniform got here, they couldn't get a response. Then they discovered the back door had been forced open, and they found him in the living room.'

She paused, turned the drink in her hands, and exhaled.

'That bad?'

She raised her chin, her mouth set straight. 'Apparently, he's had his eyes gouged out, Sarge.'

She watched as his Adam's apple bobbed once in his throat, and then he straightened his shoulders and jerked his head towards the house.

'Gillian here?'

'Got here twenty minutes ago.'

'Any sign of his—'

'Eyes? No. Not yet.'

Jan turned away, noticing the crowd of onlookers gathered at the perimeter of the crime scene.

The first responders had acted quickly, taping off an area well away from the property to avoid anyone being able to get a picture on their smartphone. The last thing they needed was for this latest murder to be broadcast on social media before they had a chance to coordinate with local news channels.

The inner cordon where she and Turpin stood was a hive of activity – instructions were being issued to crime scene investigators in muted tones, while uniformed officers took a statement from the neighbour who had raised the alarm, his face a mottled grey.

He appeared to be in a state of shock, and Jan wondered if he would stay in the area for long once the reality of the situation had sunk in. She wouldn't be surprised if his house was placed on the market within weeks, and wondered whether it would sell.

As she faced the priest's house once more, she watched the blue strobing across the rendered brickwork caused by the lights from emergency vehicles parked at the kerb next to where they stood. Through a window to the left of the front door, partially obscured by the thick material of the curtains, the flash from a photographer's camera exploded with white light.

A strong perfume wafted across, and she frowned as she tried to locate its origin before spotting the flower border bursting with hyacinths and freesias. As she ran her gaze over the landscaped front garden she was struck by a wistfulness that the place might fall to wrack and ruin.

Movement out of the corner of her eye caught her

attention, and she noticed the neighbour being ushered back to his house by one of the uniformed officers who had been speaking with him.

The front door was pushed shut, and Jan silently congratulated the young police officer for his foresight in ensuring privacy for the witness from both the investigators working the scene and the other residents who craned their necks to try and see better over the established cordon.

A moment later, one of Gillian Appleworth's colleagues peered out from behind the front door to the priest's house and beckoned to her.

'Sarge, we're wanted.'

She thanked the police constable who raised the tape for her as she ducked beneath it, scrawled her signature across the page on a clipboard the woman thrust under her nose, and then took a set of protective coveralls from a junior member of the CSI team and pulled them over her trouser suit. Booties and masks were next, and then once she and Turpin were suitably attired, he led the way up the path that bisected the tragically neat garden.

Following him over the threshold, she began to steel herself for what she expected would be a challenging crime scene. One look at the face of the younger of the first responders told her all she needed to know about the state of affairs inside the house.

'Jan, Mark.'

Gillian stood next to a door leading off from the left of the hallway, her mask pulled down to her throat and her mouth downturned.

Jan met the woman's gaze and a sense of foreboding chilled her spine. 'Are you okay?'

The pathologist shoulders straightened as she replaced her mask and led the way into the room. 'Come on through.'

Jan was immediately struck by the utter destruction.

Every picture had been torn from the wall, and as their shoes crunched across shards of glass that lay scattered across the carpet, Jan cast her eyes over the illustrations.

'He painted?'

'Looks like it. Quite good as well.'

They weaved their way past three scene of crime officers who were finalising their work, having taken the room apart piece by piece.

Jan made sure she kept to the designated path they'd cleared for ease of egress.

The priest's body lay slumped in an overstuffed armchair, a rope around his neck and a gag stuffed into his mouth. A bloody mess had congealed where his eyes had once been, and Jan shuddered as she followed Gillian around a low table in front of the chair.

Her gaze rested on the priest's hands, his fingers splayed as if he'd clawed at the armrests of the chair in an attempt to break free.

'Jesus,' she whispered.

'His killer left the rope behind this time,' said Mark. 'Why?'

Gillian peered over her mask at him. 'Because it's cut so deep into the skin, I doubt it could have been pulled out quickly.'

'Fingerprints?' Mark turned his attention to the crime scene investigator who crouched next to the body.

'Perhaps,' came the muffled reply. 'Partials, at least. As with the last murder, it appears our killer wore some sort of thin gloves. Not enough to hide his prints completely, but enough to make sure we can't get a decent sample.'

Mark turned his attention back to the vandalised room. 'There's more rage in this murder than Seamus's, isn't there? I mean, last time the killer didn't hang around. This—'

'It's almost like he wasn't in control,' said Jan. She turned to Jasper Smith, who was supervising the CSI team. 'Do you think he killed the priest first, and then trashed the room?'

'We'll know for sure once we've put together our report,' he said, 'but there are shards of glass down the side of the priest's body, which suggests the pictures were destroyed afterwards and the glass showered over him.'

'Okay, thanks. We'll get out of your way,' said Mark, as he turned to leave.

Jan went to follow him, then paused as Gillian held up her hand.

'His name was Philip, by the way. Philip Baxter. We found his wallet on the side table over there.'

'Thank you.'

'Always makes it more personal when you know their names, doesn't it?'

'True,' said Jan. 'And there's something very personal about these murders.'

CHAPTER NINETEEN

Mark ran his hand over his eyes, and silently thanked the fact he hadn't finished the second beer.

Fatigue was starting to set in, a clear indication that his body still hadn't adjusted.

He waited while Jan knocked on the neighbour's door, then followed her once the young police constable let them in and ran his gaze over the photographs hanging on the hallway walls.

The couple who lived there were evidently retired, and doted on their grandchildren. Each photograph depicted a family gathering over the years as the children had grown, corralled into portraits that marked time passing.

PC John Newton introduced himself and brought them up to date with the witness statement he'd taken.

'His wife's out at the moment,' he said. 'Should be back any minute, according to him.'

Mark skim-read PC Newton's notes, then handed them back to the young officer.

'Thank you. They're very thorough.'

'Thanks. Do you want to talk to him?'

'Yes, I wouldn't mind. Is he through there?'

'In the kitchen. Don't have a cup of tea if he offers to make you one, though.'

Mark frowned. 'Dirty cups?'

'No – piss weak.'

Mark heard Jan snort, and then led the way over the threshold and along the hallway to the kitchen.

He wrinkled his nose at the trail of damp across the ceiling of the hallway, and then glanced down as Jan tapped his shoulder and indicated he should follow her.

A blue fug greeted him as he entered the kitchen, and it took all his self-control not to begin clearing his throat the moment he was introduced to John Keswick.

He'd noticed the stench of cigarettes as they'd entered the house and spoken with PC Newton, but in here it was almost unbearable. He blinked to try and stop his eyes from stinging and resisted the urge to retreat.

Instead, he took in the yellow tinge to the man's fingernails as they shook hands, and wondered if it'd be rude to ask him for a glass of water. He discounted the idea immediately, and instead gestured to Jan to lead the interview.

'Mr Keswick, we realise you've already spoken with our colleagues regarding the events of this evening,' she began, 'but we'd like to ask a few more questions.'

The man grunted in response and waved them to a dining table off to one side of the kitchen, a newspaper spread open at the local sports section and an ashtray close by.

'Have a seat.'

'That's okay, we'll stand – thanks.' She glanced at Mark, and he raised a hand in response.

The urge to choke had subsided.

'Mr Keswick, do you know of anyone that would want to harm Father Baxter?' he said.

'No.' The man shook his head, and shoved his hands into the pockets of his trousers, but not before Mark noticed Keswick's hands trembling.

'What about visitors lately? Noticed anyone?'

He received a shrug by way of response.

'No-one at all?'

'Not really, no. I tend to spend my time in here mostly, you see. Wendy doesn't like me smoking in the front room.'

'That's your wife, yes?'

'Yes.'

'And where is she at the moment?'

'Book club. At the library.'

'What time did she leave?'

Keswick blew a low whistle as he contemplated the ceiling. 'Ooh, I don't know. About quarter to seven, I suppose. Takes about twenty minutes from here, but she likes to get there early to set up the chairs.'

'And she's due back...?'

'Any time soon. She was going to call in to the supermarket on the way home. They're open late tonight.'

'Did she drive?'

'No – doesn't like driving these days. One of her friends from the club collects her, and then drops her off after they've done the shopping.'

'Okay, so do you wave her off, or anything like that?'

'No – why would I?'

'You didn't see anyone hanging around in the lane this evening?'

'Like I said, I've been in here all night – until I heard the shouting.'

'And when was that?'

'About an hour and a half after she left. I was going to wander through and put the telly on – there's a programme I like to watch on one of the history

channels. Boats and the like. That's when I heard it –
some sort of commotion.'

'What exactly did you hear?'

'A crash – like a door had been forced, or
something had fallen over. Something heavy, because it
shook the walls. Then shouting.' He emitted a shaking
sigh. 'Then it went quiet, and that's when I got
worried. I mean, he lives on his own, doesn't he? And I
didn't hear any cars pull up outside before that, so I
couldn't understand what was going on.'

'Is that when you dialled triple nine?'

'Yes. But then I worried they wouldn't get here in
time if it was urgent. I've read about the budget cuts.'

Mark grimaced. 'You should've stayed in your
house, Mr Keswick. It could've been incredibly
dangerous for you.'

'I realise that now after seeing... after—'

Mark gave him a moment, and then continued.
'Did Baxter seem troubled by anything of late?'

Keswick ran a hand over his jawline. 'Come to
think of it, he did. We used to pass the time of day if we
saw each other in the garden, see?'

'Can you elaborate?'

He shrugged. 'It might've been nothing, I suppose,
but last week we were having a chat over the back
fence when his mobile phone rang. It's so quiet around
here we could hear it from outside. Always made me

chuckle because it's the theme tune from *Mission Impossible*.' His smile faded as quickly as it had appeared. 'The thing was, he fair jumped out of his skin. He looked terrified, and when I asked him if he needed to answer it, he said he didn't. Said it was better if it went to voicemail. Couldn't understand that, him being a priest and all. I mean, what if it was urgent and someone needed their last rites?'

'Did you ask him if something was troubling him?'

'I did, but he wouldn't tell me. I wondered if maybe someone had told him something and it worried him. Wendy called me indoors just after that – she had our lunch ready. When I asked Father Baxter if everything was alright, he said he'd be fine. I wasn't convinced, so I said I'd be happy to pop round later that afternoon, but he said not to bother because he wouldn't be able to tell me anyway.'

'What do you mean?'

Keswick shrugged. 'Well, he's Catholic, isn't he?'

'What's that got to do with it?'

'Well, I suppose if someone tells him something in the confessional, he can't go offloading that knowledge to anyone else, can he?'

CHAPTER TWENTY

Mark woke early, the sound of the bells from St Nicholas jerking him from his sleep.

He couldn't remember the nightmare, he never could, but it left him with a sense of unease that he knew would only subside with physical labour.

Electing to clean the narrowboat from bow to stern, he immersed himself in washing the gunwales, scrubbing mould from the outer windowsills and polishing every brass fastening and ornament in sight.

Sweat poured from his brow as he worked his way around the vessel, his aching muscles a constant reminder of what his body had endured. He ignored the tension between his shoulders, and pushed away the memories that threatened to surface.

Hamish sat on the towpath with a look of bemusement on his face at Mark's efforts, then scampered away with an excited bark after a group of walkers further across the meadow. He grew bored once they disappeared from sight heading towards the town, and returned to curl up on the deck as it warmed from the sun.

Satisfied the boat was cleaner than when he'd first moved in, Mark eyed the boxes on the seats in the cabin.

The thought of rummaging through the contents of his life left a sour taste in his mouth, and, despite the novelty of being on the boat, he intended to be back on land prior to winter setting in.

He would deal with the boxes then, not before.

Instead, and by the time his watch showed six-thirty, Mark had showered, put fresh water in a bowl for Hamish and set off for work, his mind calmer.

An hour later, he glanced up as a plate was shoved under his nose, a ham and cheese toasted sandwich placed squarely in the middle that sent his senses into overdrive.

'Eat,' said Jan and grinned. 'I swear it's like having a third kid to look after.'

'Thanks. I didn't realise what the time was.'

'What time did you get in this morning? I saw you were here when I arrived.'

'About seven. Thought I'd try to get a head start.'

'Do you sleep?'

It was his turn to smile. 'Occasionally,' he said, then sank his teeth into the corner of the sandwich.

'What happened last night?'

'What do you mean?'

In response, Jan pointed at her throat. 'When we were at Keswick's house. You looked like you couldn't breathe. Given your voice sounds damaged, I wondered why. Obviously the smoky atmosphere affected you for a moment there.'

Mark dropped his sandwich onto the plate, his appetite fading. He saw no sense in denying Jan the truth – after all, they'd be working together for the foreseeable future.

'Back in Swindon, I got throttled by a suspect. After he stabbed me.'

Her eyes opened wide. 'Oh. So, the smoke aggravated the damage to your throat?'

'Yeah. Anything like that can make me feel like I'm struggling for air.'

'Sorry.'

He forced a smile. 'Not your fault.'

'No, but I'll be mindful of it in future. If I'd known that, I'd have offered to speak to him on my own.' She glanced over her shoulder as DI Kennedy entered the incident room, then pointed at the sandwich he'd abandoned. 'Finish that. We can't have you fainting on the job.'

She winked and then made her way over to her own desk, and he eyed up the food before snatching it up and devouring it in four mouthfuls.

She was right – he was famished.

He dusted crumbs from his trousers and joined Kennedy as he weaved between the crush of desks to the whiteboard at the end of the room.

Despite the seriousness of the case, the DI had only managed to coerce a small increase to his budget from the Chief Superintendent to assure overtime for a skeleton staff at the weekend, and so a reduced number of officers gathered for the briefing.

'Thanks to everyone for giving up your Saturday mornings. What's the latest from the CSIs?' said Kennedy as a uniformed officer handed him a mug of coffee. 'Thanks, Simon.'

'Jasper Smith confirms the killer broke in, guv,' said Jan. 'Whoever attacked Philip Baxter wasn't put off by the new locks on the doors. Jasper reckons he used a crowbar or something.'

'Yet when Seamus was killed, his attacker waited until he was unable to hear him approach,' said Mark. 'Our killer's getting bolder.'

'You think it's the same killer?'

He shrugged in response. 'It's what we're all thinking, isn't it?'

A hubbub of agreement filtered amongst the group.

'Did anyone think to check where Terry Benedict was last night?' said Kennedy, bringing everyone's attention back to the agenda at hand.

'Guv. Says he was working between six o'clock and nine last night,' said McClellan. 'He checks out – he was serving behind the bar. Busy night in Upper Benham, by all accounts – he says most of the talk in the pub last night was about Seamus's death. He only left the bar at one point to help out in the kitchen. Both the girls working behind the bar and the kitchen staff support his statement.'

'Okay, thanks.' Kennedy drew a question mark next to Benedict's photograph on the whiteboard. 'In that case, if we *are* looking for a single killer, that could lift the suspicion on him for Seamus's murder. We're leaving nothing to chance, though, in case there's an accomplice involved.'

A murmur swept the group.

'Next – we've got a media conference lined up for three o'clock this afternoon. We won't be drawing parallels between the two murders until all the evidence is logged from last night's scene and we have Gillian's post mortem report, but you can bet the rumours are going to start once this gets out. We're keeping an embargo on specific information relating to both murders, namely the eye gouging and Seamus being relieved of his tongue. For now, we need to

establish if there's a connection between Seamus and
Baxter, so Jan – work with McClellan and get onto the
diocese again.'

'Guv.'

'Mark – I'd like you at the media conference later
today. Don't worry, I'll do all the talking. I want a show
of strength, though. Last thing we want is to give the
impression to the public we're not doing all we can
with the manpower we've got.'

'Got it.'

'All right. That's it for now. If anything changes or
you receive vital information over the course of today,
let me know. Otherwise, we'll have another briefing
once everyone else is here on Monday morning.'

Mark reached out his hand as Jan passed, pulling
her to a standstill.

'What's up?' she said.

'I reckon we should have another word with Terry
Benedict.'

'Why?'

'I was thinking about Seamus, and the fact
Benedict said he was approached from time to time
while he was having a drink at the pub. I wonder if he
met anyone there rather than his house or the church
who might be able to shed some light on the murders.'

'We're definitely working on the premise that
they're somehow linked, then?'

'I think so, don't you? I think we should at least ask Benedict if Seamus had been speaking to someone there – whether that's someone local or a stranger that he might have noticed.'

She took a gulp of coffee, and then nodded. 'Okay. Monday, then?'

'Yeah. After the morning briefing. Maybe by then we'll have some more information from Gillian that'll help us.'

CHAPTER TWENTY-ONE

Jan turned her attention from her computer screen as McClellan approached her desk, a thin collection of paperwork in his hands and a despondent expression in his eyes.

'I've printed out everything we've received so far from the diocesan office,' he said, 'but don't get your hopes up.'

'Like that, is it? Ten per cent useful, and the rest of it bullshit?'

He managed a smile. 'Pretty much.'

'Okay, give me that lot and bring a chair over. Let's see what you've got.'

She flicked through the assorted documents while McClellan rolled a chair across the thin carpet, and then pushed her keyboard out of the way and spread out the pages.

The detective constable had ended his probationary period six months ago, but she sensed he still struggled with having confidence in his own abilities.

She couldn't help herself – with two young boys at home, she found herself attempting to draw the young man out of the shell he had created in order to survive the often brash culture that could take over the incident room sometimes.

'Do you want to give me your first impressions?' she said.

'Well, I went through the two emails they sent over this afternoon. One of those was in relation to the request you sent asking for clarification as to why Seamus Carter was transferred from Bristol to here. They say that the priest who was at Upper Benham at the time – Magnus Taylor – was in ill health, and they wanted to establish someone new in the community before he retired so that people had a chance to get used to Carter while he worked alongside him.'

'Is the old priest still around?

'No – he died a few years ago. I spoke with the man's sister, but she said he didn't leave much by way of belongings or documentation about his time in the village. Unfortunately, she didn't keep any of it.'

Jan frowned, and ran her finger down the page.

'What about the background checks and employment history that Kennedy asked you to get a hold of?'

'They came through late yesterday – here you go.' He paused as Jan began to read. 'There's nothing in that to suggest he was in trouble or anything.'

She snorted, and put the stapled pages to one side. 'Lots of praise, and not much else, as you say. What about the diaries and address book that Jasper's lot bagged up from Carter's house? Anything in those?'

McClellan shook his head. 'I worked through the address book with Caroline, and we've accounted for everyone in there. It was mostly local people, contacts he had at the diocesan office, and things like that.'

'Anything from his time in the parish near Bristol?'

'No, but the address book didn't seem that old. I suppose if he bought a new one, he wouldn't have bothered transposing over anyone's details he wasn't in contact with anymore. I know my nan doesn't with hers.' He gave a sad smile. 'She's always saying that she spends more time crossing out dead people than adding new names these days.'

'Bless her.' Jan placed the address book on the growing pile of documents they'd discounted. 'And the diaries?'

'Just church stuff – you know, weddings, fundraising activities, that sort of thing.'

'Okay.' Jan sighed and pointed at the other

documents. 'Is there anything amongst what the diocesan office sent through about Carter knowing Philip Baxter?'

'Not that I could find. I mean, Baxter might've been in a different parish, I suppose, but he definitely wasn't at the same one as Carter.'

She groaned. 'Christ, it's like pulling teeth. I told them I wanted a list of names for the whole of that diocese, not just the parish Carter was based at prior to coming here. How hard can it be?'

'Do you want me to chase them up in the morning?'

'Please. Mark wants to head back to the pub to speak to Terry Benedict, and I'd like to keep on top of this lot.'

'What's he like to work with?'

'Who? Mark?'

'Yes. Caroline said he was involved in a big case in Swindon before he came here.'

'I'd imagine he's worked on a lot of big cases, Alex. He's got to be ten years older than you. Give it a few more years, and you'll be racking them up. Unfortunately.'

The younger detective's mouth twisted as he stood and began to gather up the paperwork. 'It's like that, isn't it? I mean, I want to learn more and get more experience, but in a horrible way that means something bad has to happen to someone in order for me to do that.'

'It's the way it goes,' she said. 'But that's why we do what we do, right?'

'I suppose.' His gaze drifted to Mark's abandoned desk, the DS having left half an hour ago to prepare for the media conference. 'He's confident, isn't he?

'That's just experience. The more you do this, the more you've got to draw upon the next time something similar crops up.' She gestured to the whiteboard at the end of the incident room. 'And trust me, this one has us all scratching our heads.'

He turned back to her. 'So, what's he like to work with then?'

'Not bad. Tidier than you, for a start.' She winked. 'I'm sure you'll get the chance to work with him at some point, given that he seems to be here on a permanent basis.'

McClellan's eyes lit up. 'Really? That would be great.'

Jan laughed. 'He's a detective sergeant, not a rock star.'

CHAPTER TWENTY-TWO

Mark held up a hand and grimaced as another two press photographers held up their cameras, the bright flashes searing his vision before he could shield his eyes.

The large room was crowded with so many people that all of the chairs had been taken within the first ten minutes of the doors opening, and two of the administrative staff battled with one of the sliding partition walls to allow more television camera operators to set up along the side of the assembled gathering.

The hubbub of conversation grew louder, and Mark reached out for the glass of water on the table in front of him while he tried to concentrate on his breathing.

The low ceiling seemed to encroach upon the

space, and he resisted the urge to rest the cool glass against his forehead.

Instead, he forced a smile as he heard his name above the racket and turned to his left, where DI Kennedy sat talking with Sarah from the media relations office in muted tones as she ran through last-minute amendments to the prepared statement.

'I was just saying, perhaps we should let you answer some of the questions,' said Kennedy, oblivious to Mark's discomfort. 'I said I wanted a show of force, and Sarah thinks it'd be a good opportunity to display the sort of experience we have available to this investigation. You okay with that?'

'Of course,' said Mark.

Like I have a choice.

He turned back to face the reporters.

Sweeping his gaze across the various news channel logos he could see affixed to microphones and the sides of the television cameras, he wondered if any Swindon-based journalists had nipped over the border to cover the story.

Until that afternoon, he had hoped to maintain the low profile he had kept since his recuperation.

All he wanted was to be left alone to do his job. To find out who had murdered two priests, and why.

Not this.

He bit back an exasperated sigh as Sarah moved

away from Kennedy and took up position beside a back door leading from the room, and fought an impulse to dash through it.

The DI was right – they needed to demonstrate that they were doing all they could to solve this case.

Squaring his shoulders as Sarah called out a ten-second warning for the waiting throng, he cleared his throat and listened while Kennedy read out the statement.

'We can confirm that last night, between the hours of seven and eight o'clock, Father Philip Baxter was murdered in his home at St Martin's Meadow. At the present time, we cannot confirm any link between his death and that of Seamus Carter last weekend. Our enquiries are ongoing, and we would ask all members of the public to contact us with any information that may help with the investigation.'

Mark tuned out the DI's words as his gaze scanned the assembled throng and wondered if any of them believed Kennedy's insistence that the two murders were not somehow connected.

He could already imagine tomorrow's headlines.

A hush remained, save for the occasional vibration from a silenced mobile phone, and all eyes were trained on the man beside him.

He wondered if the priests' killer was watching the live broadcast.

Would he be congratulating himself on the lack of progress in the hunt for Carter's killer and a second murder?

Was he already planning to kill again?

And why?

He blinked to clear the thought as Kennedy fell silent for a moment after finishing the statement, and then all hell broke loose as the DI invited questions from the impatient journalists.

A forest of raised hands and shouted calls for attention filled the air, until Kennedy singled out an older woman at the front of the room.

'Diane?'

'You say that you can't confirm a link between the two murders at the moment, but *are* you looking for one killer?'

'We cannot confirm that at the present time,' said Kennedy. 'When we have more information to hand, we'll let you know in that regard.'

The hands shot up again.

Kennedy gestured to a reporter towards the back of the room.

The man stood, notebook in hand, and used his pen to point in Mark's direction.

'Detective Turpin, you were previously based in Swindon and have only just returned to work after an extended leave of absence. Are you fit enough to be involved in a double murder investigation?'

Mark's heartbeat lurched a split second before he heard blood rushing in his ears. He reached forward to adjust the microphone, and cleared his throat.

'Detective Inspector Kennedy specifically requested my presence on this investigating team because of the experience I bring to the role,' he said, his voice little more than a growl.

'But can you?' The reporter gave a predatory smile. 'After all, your last case nearly ended in personal tragedy, and—'

Kennedy leaned forward. 'I'll remind you all to keep your questions relevant to the investigation at hand.'

He pointed to a man standing beside one of the television cameras, his mobile phone held out while he recorded proceedings. 'Yes?'

'Two priests dead in the space of a week,' said the journalist, unable to keep the eagerness from his voice. 'Are there going to be more?'

'Really, I think that's the sort of sensationalism that shouldn't be reported,' said Kennedy, his jaw tightening. 'We're talking about two men who had their lives brutally cut short in horrific circumstances.'

'But what about other priests in the area?' called a woman from the back of the room. 'Are they safe?'

'We've asked all religious organisations to advise their members to take additional safety precautions when alone,' said Kennedy. 'They have assured us that they will be working with their communities to make sure that message is adhered to.'

Mark gritted his teeth as the DI fielded questions for another five minutes, and then drew the press conference to a close.

'Thank you, everyone, for your time,' said Kennedy.

He pushed back his chair and both men followed Sarah through the door and into a corridor beyond.

Mark stumbled as the media officer closed the door, and leaned against the wall, running his palm across his forehead.

'Do you think all that will help?' he said.

Kennedy's lips thinned. 'I bloody hope so. We haven't got much else to go on, have we?'

CHAPTER TWENTY-THREE

The next morning, Mark left Hamish prowling the towpath beside his boat and then set off towards the centre of town.

By the time he reached the main road at Bridge Street, a stiff breeze was blowing and he was glad he had slipped a jacket over his shoulders before departing the boat.

He glanced at the church to his right as he strolled along Market Place, but it wasn't the one he sought.

He checked his watch, and then picked up his pace. On reaching the boat last night, he had powered up his laptop to find the website and check the times.

Part of him was surprised that the service was held mid-morning, fully expecting an early start. Instead, he'd had a leisurely breakfast and attempted to sort through two of the boxes in the cabin before setting off.

The brisk walk would do him good, he knew. He had spent much of the time off work concentrating on the exercises the physiotherapist had given him, returning to the gym as soon as possible. With the move from Wiltshire, however, his routine had been in danger of falling by the wayside and he resolved to explore more of the towpath with Hamish once the current investigation was concluded.

At the end of the street, he turned right and followed the busy road towards a roundabout in the distance. He spotted the spire of the church, towering into the sky about it.

It always struck him how modern Catholic churches appeared compared to the Church of England buildings. The Reformation had destroyed most, and from the scant research he had conducted the previous night over a glass of wine, he had learned that the church had been completed in the nineteenth century.

A path led from the main road through lush grass and around the side of the building to the front doors.

Organ music played, welcoming worshippers as they drifted in for the morning Mass.

Pausing at the archway that created a porch, he peered through the open double doors. He could see no-one, but muted voices reached him from within.

He turned at footsteps to see an elderly gentleman approaching, and stepped to one side.

'Good morning,' said the man. 'First time here?'

'Is it that obvious?'

The man smiled. 'It's only a small congregation, but friendly. I tend to know the familiar faces, if not the names.'

Mark relaxed a little. 'I was passing by.'

'Well, you're welcome to come in.'

'I'm not religious. I mean, sorry. I was curious, that's all.'

'As are most of us. There's nothing to worry about – if you want to sit at the back and watch, no-one will mind.'

'Thank you, I'll do that.'

He followed the man over the threshold, and stood for a moment admiring the vaulted ceilings and the dappled light through ornate stained-glass windows. A familiar mustiness reached his senses, the same scent of old books and history that he had noticed in the church at Upper Benham, despite the modernity of his surroundings.

Movement to the left of where he stood caught his attention, and noticing a priest emerging from a room at the back and heading for the altar, Mark slipped into a pew at the back of the congregation.

As the service began, he wondered how the

parishioners knew when to respond to the priest's incantations, and then noticed a thin card that had been placed on the shelf of the pew in front.

He reached out for it, and cast his eyes down the text, realising it was a running order and that the parishioners who weren't familiar with the Mass could follow it.

He went to replace it, but it slipped from his grasp and tumbled to the floor. Red-faced, he gave up trying to retrieve it and instead craned his neck to see around the people sitting a few rows ahead of his position to find out what was going on.

To his surprise, the priest finished and took a seat behind the altar.

At once, a man rose from a pew at the front, and began to speak.

As Mark let the words wash over him, he realised he recognised the passage from the Bible, the reading interspersed with the congregation calling "Amen" at regular intervals.

When the speaker had finished, the priest moved until he was standing behind the altar once more, and announced he'd be reading from the gospel of St John.

Eventually, he turned his attention to a pewter goblet and lifted a thin wafer from a plate, held it aloft, then raised the chalice and took a sip. When he was done, a steady stream of parishioners flocked to the front of the church to accept their wafer from the priest.

Mark edged out of his pew and scurried towards the open doors, not stopping until he reached the far end of the path by the main road.

The sun was reaching its zenith by now, and he shrugged his jacket off his shoulders, draped it across one arm and crossed the grass to a wooden bench that had been placed under a group of trees a little way from the path.

He monitored the scant congregation as they left the church, each taking the priest's hand in their own before exchanging a few words.

Some left in pairs, others alone, and he spotted the old man that had invited him inside, acknowledging him with a nod as he passed.

'Enjoy the rest of your Sunday.'

'Thanks. You too.'

Mark watched until the crowd had dispersed, then leaned forward and rested his elbows on his knees, resisting the urge to hold his head in his hands.

How do you feel? the psychiatrist appointed to him would have asked if she were beside him.

Unsettled, he thought. *Confused, and unsettled.*

Why would anyone kill two priests?

CHAPTER TWENTY-FOUR

When Mark reached the top of the staircase that led to the incident room the following morning, the first thing that struck him was the amount of noise emanating through the door that had been left ajar.

He checked his watch, paranoid that he had slept in, but it was definitely half past seven.

He hurried forward and shoved the door open to see Alex McClellan standing at the far end of the room, a pile of paper plates in his hand.

McClellan waved him over and thrust one of the plates at him.

'Thanks. What's going on?'

Jan glanced over her shoulder from where she was leaning over a desk and smiled. She gestured at the array of pastries and cake slices that took up most of its surface.

'It's my birthday. Got a plate? Good – give it here. If you don't get in quick, you'll miss out.'

'It's your birthday? Why didn't you say anything? I didn't get you anything.'

'It's all right. No big deal. We only ever do cakes, anyway.'

'It's May, though.'

She frowned. 'I know.'

'But, you're called January.'

'Only by my mother. And not since I was thirteen. Unless Jasper is trying to wind me up.'

'Huh. Ironic. Happy birthday.' He gestured towards the whiteboard. 'Is Kennedy here?'

'Arrived ten minutes ago. I think he's about to start the briefing.'

Mark took his plate over to his desk, shrugged off his coat and folded it over the back of his chair, then sat and switched on his computer while taking a bite from the Danish pastry.

He swept crumbs from the desk, typed in his password and ran his gaze over the emails that had accumulated since Saturday.

A whole swathe were from the personnel team, instructing him to sign documents, read policies and procedures pertaining to the station, and requesting he report to the IT team to collect a permanent security card. He blanched at the sight of a request for his attendance at an induction workshop, figuring that, as he'd already been at the station for a week, he could probably run that himself, and then looked up from the screen as DI Kennedy swept into view.

'Happy birthday, Jan,' he said as he strode over to the whiteboard.

'Thanks, guv.'

'Right – let's get this out of the way.' Kennedy held up a report in his hand. 'Gillian's sent through her report, so I'll run through the salient points, and then you can get back to work.'

Mark pushed back his chair and joined the throng at the far end of the room, wiping his fingers on a napkin as the first throes of the sugar rush hit his system.

'Right, so for those of you who weren't in over the weekend, I'll give you a potted history of our second victim,' said Kennedy, pushing his reading glasses up his nose. 'Philip Baxter. Aged sixty-four. Moved around over the years, but has been the parish priest for St Martin's Meadow for the past ten years. Witness statements taken on Friday night and over the weekend from neighbours and parishioners give the impression he was well respected in the community.'

He paused while he shuffled the documentation in his hands and turned to the back page of Gillian's post mortem report. 'Evidently our pathologist deemed our case important enough to conduct her examination over the weekend, so here's what you need to know. As with Seamus Carter, Baxter was restrained by a rope that was looped over his head and around his neck, restricting air flow. According to Gillian, Baxter put up a fight – there are traces of his blood in the rope fibres consistent with that found under his fingernails. She's spoken to the CSI lead, who confirms the ends of the rope were left draped over the back of the armchair, so the killer trod on those to keep the rope taut while he gouged out Baxter's eyes.'

A murmur swept the room, and the DI cleared his throat.

'I didn't say it made for pleasant reading, did I? We'll have the full report and recommendations from the CSIs tomorrow at the latest. Caroline – can you follow up and ensure all the evidence collated on Friday night is logged?'

'Guv.'

'If it isn't, grab someone from uniform to give you a hand – I want that database up to date by lunchtime.'

'Will do.'

'Next, motive. It doesn't look like anything was stolen from the property, and so it appears that he was targeted.'

'Are we working on the presumption it's the same

killer?' said a uniformed officer towards the back of the group.

'Indeed we are, given the fact that once again our victim is missing some body parts, as well as being a priest. As you'll have seen from Saturday's televised statement, we aren't broadcasting that to the press, is that understood?' Kennedy flicked the whiteboard marker pen between his fingers. 'I think it's quite clear to all of us that there's an enormous amount of rage in these two murders. So, what did our priests do? Why were they targeted? Why now?'

'Could it be about abuse?' said McClellan. 'Revenge for something like that could be a motive if the killer was abused in the past by the victims of these murders. Maybe he's got frustrated with the legal system and taken matters into his own hands.'

Kennedy wrote the suggestion on the whiteboard. 'Why take Seamus's tongue and Baxter's eyes? What's the point of doing that?'

He continued, not waiting for a response. 'Finally – no-one saw Baxter's killer leave the house. The neighbour, John Keswick, reported hearing a noise, so he phoned triple nine. Curiosity got the better of him before uniform arrived, and he had a key to the priest's house – apparently he watered the garden when Baxter was away for any length of time.' Kennedy dropped Gillian's report onto the desk beside him and folded his arms. 'No doubt by now, he's realising how lucky he was that our murderer took flight rather than confronting him. I have a feeling we'd be looking at another victim otherwise. As it was, Keswick reported the back door was open when he entered the hallway through the front door. There's a field bordering the properties on Marsh Lane, and it looks like that was our killer's method of escape. The CSIs have processed the area, but apart from a partial footprint haven't found anything else to assist us.'

He turned his attention to the whiteboard, updated the bullet points under each victim's photographs, then re-capped the pen and called over his shoulder.

'Jan – you mentioned you and Mark wanted to speak to the landlord of the White Horse at Upper Benham again. What's your thinking with that one?'

Mark stepped forward as Jan turned to him. 'We want to find out if Seamus was approached by anyone at the time he was in the pub having a drink – a stranger, or someone not usually seen at the church. Plus, we'll take a photograph of Philip Baxter with us, in case Terry Benedict recognises him. It's a long shot, I know—'

'But worth following up, as you say. Okay, good.'

Mark leaned against a colleague's desk as the DI worked his way around the encircled team, giving instructions and listening to feedback from the inquiry to date, then dismissed them and returned to his office.

As the team dispersed, he joined Jan at her desk as she gathered up her bag and car keys before they made their way towards the door.

She frowned as he held it open for her. 'What if our murderer hasn't finished? What if he's planning to kill again?'

'Can't rule anything out at the moment, Jan. Best hope we catch him before he does.'

CHAPTER TWENTY-FIVE

A steady downpour had set in by the time Mark followed Jan out to the car park.

She dashed over to the pool car, threw her umbrella onto the back seat and started the engine as he opened the door, the vents in front of the windscreen on full blast while she tried to clear the condensation.

'Why does it always have to rain when the boys have PE?' she said. 'I was hoping to get away with not having to do laundry after work tonight.'

He smiled, recalling the days he would collect his daughters from school with damp clothes bundled into school bags that would bear the stench for days afterwards, but said nothing.

Instead, he settled in for the ride as Jan pointed the car towards Upper Benham, the traffic lighter now that the commuter rush of the morning had passed, and he spent the journey consulting his notes from the morning briefing.

The car park of the White Horse had turned into a quagmire by the time she braked next to the side entrance to the pub, and Mark glanced across at the boundary in the hedgerow that led to the church.

Any remaining evidence would be washed away by now, but he had a feeling the team of CSIs wouldn't have discovered anything further.

Their killer had been too well prepared.

He held open the door for Jan, then followed her through the maze of tables and chairs to the bar where Terry Benedict stood chatting to an older man perched on a stool.

A mottled greyhound clambered to its feet as they approached, and he held out his hand for the ageing dog to sniff.

'She's friendly,' said the man.

Mark smiled. 'Most greyhounds are, aren't they?'

'What can I do for you, detectives?' said Benedict, reaching out for a glass and polishing it with a tea towel that had been draped over his shoulder.

'Mind if we have a quick word?'

'I'm serving at the moment. I'm here on my own until six o'clock.'

Mark raised an eyebrow. 'It won't take long.'

'Go on, Terry. I'll keep an eye on the bar,' said the older man, and took a sip from his pint. 'I'll give you a shout if anyone comes in.'

Resigned, the landlord pointed at a table some way from the bar. 'Have a seat, then.'

Mark waited until they'd settled, and then held out the photograph of Philip Baxter taken from his personnel file provided by the diocesan office that had been chosen for the media release over the weekend.

'Recognise this man?'

'Is this the other priest who I heard was killed?'

'Yes. Did you ever see him and Seamus together?'

'No. Not in here, nor over at the church – mind you, I wasn't a regular visitor over there. Not Catholic, see?'

'We've got a list of your regulars who were here that Saturday night, as well as some other people who were known to you and your staff, but was there anyone who you hadn't seen before you might have gotten a name for?'

Benedict lowered his gaze and stared at the floor. After a moment, he held up his index finger. 'Only a couple of them – I think they knew the band, or liked their music, something like that. Anyway, they seemed to follow them around to various gigs because each of them went up to the little stage we set up in the corner over there and spoke to them at one time or another

during the evening. One was a bloke in his late fifties –
Jerry, I think I heard the guitarist call him. The other
was a woman who obviously had a thing for the singer.
Got too drunk by the end of the evening, slurring her
words and draping herself all over Tom Castle who
runs a local joinery business – not that I heard him
complaining, mind. I think her name was Angela, but
I'm not sure.'

'No last names?'

'No, sorry – I'm lucky if I get to hear their first
names sometimes, what with the music and people
shouting over it most of the time.'

'What about the band? Where were they from?'

'Oxford's their usual haunt, although they're good,
so they get gigs up and down the country. I'm lucky if I
manage to book them once every six months. Wish I
could get them more often – I'm always guaranteed a
good night's takings when they're here.'

Mark turned in his seat and surveyed the corner
where Benedict said he'd set up the stage, then
frowned.

'How the hell do you squash a band into there?' he
said. He glanced over his shoulder to see the landlord
smiling at him. 'What?'

'They're a duo. Backing tracks, see? Saves me
getting a full licence, too, but I tell you what – they
really are bloody good. Toby is the guitarist and

keyboard player. Dean is the singer. Looks the part, too.' He grinned. 'All the local girls love him.'

'No trouble that night while they were playing?'

'No trouble full stop. Wouldn't stand for it.' Benedict leaned back in his seat and crossed his arms. 'More than my business is worth, see? No – I'm careful with the bands I get in here. Toby and Dean are one of the more popular ones.'

'What do they do when they're not breaking hearts all over Oxfordshire?'

'I don't know. Never talked about it, to be honest. I deal with Toby when I want to book them – I think he's the more business savvy of the two. Dean tends to float about, even when they're setting up. I get the impression he's happy to turn up and sing, then clear off with his share of the cash. Fair enough, I suppose. If I had a voice like that, I'd probably do the same.'

'Professionally trained, is he?'

Benedict laughed. 'Not quite. According to Toby, Dean was head choir boy at a church near Bristol before he moved to Oxfordshire.'

Mark ignored the look that Jan shot him, and narrowed his eyes. 'I'd like the phone numbers for them, please.'

'I only have Toby's number. Like I said, I deal with him when I want to book them. Actually, if you see him, give him these for me, would you?' He walked back to the bar, reached into the till, and handed over two plastic plectrums, a lion embossed on one side of each. 'The cleaner found them the morning after their gig and I don't think these are the cheap ones.'

'Great,' said Mark, under his breath. 'Now I'm a bloody roadie as well.'

CHAPTER TWENTY-SIX

Mark paced the pavement at the end of a street lined with terraced houses off the Abingdon Road, and ended his phone call.

The afternoon briefing was due to start at half past five, and he was determined to follow up the lead Terry Benedict had given them before returning to the incident room.

The clatter of heels on concrete reached his ears, and he turned to see Jan hurrying towards him, shoving the car keys into her handbag as she drew near.

'Bloody parking,' she said. 'I ended up on the next street over – it's wall-to-wall cars along here.'

He waited while she caught her breath, and then jerked his thumb over his shoulder.

'The guitarist's house is down there on the left-hand side. Caroline's just phoned to confirm the car outside is registered in his name, so I'm presuming he's in.'

'Okay.' She adjusted the handbag strap over her shoulder, and then fell into step a little behind him, the pavement being too narrow for them to walk side by side. 'What did Toby say when you phoned him?'

'That he was on his way up to Birmingham for a gig tomorrow night.'

'Think he's telling the truth?'

'We'll soon find out.'

'How come you didn't just ask him for Dean's phone number?'

'I want to see his face when I do. You know what it's like – people can give away a lot by their expressions, and I want the chance to interview him properly.'

A shallow front garden led to the front door, a paved area in place of any lawn or ornamental garden like some of the neighbouring properties displayed.

'Renting, then.'

'You think so?'

'Has a temporary feel about it, doesn't it? Look at the paintwork on the windowsills – it's all chipped.'

'Maybe he hates decorating. Scott has a lot of customers like that.'

'Fair point.' He reached out and pressed the doorbell, noting the new lock that had been fitted recently, and then took a step back as a figure appeared through the mottled glass panel.

A man in his mid-twenties with floppy blond hair peered around the crack in the door, a brass chain preventing him from opening it further.

'Yes?'

'Toby Hopkins?'

'Yes. You're the copper I spoke to, yeah?'

'That's right. Can we come in?'

'Can I see your ID?'

Mark held up his warrant card, waited while Toby ran his eyes over the lettering and then retreated and closed the door.

The sound of the chain rattling against the wooden surface reached him, and then Toby opened the door wide.

'Sorry – can't be too careful around here. Insurance and stuff. A lot of the equipment I've got here costs a fortune. Come on through. Close the door behind you.'

Mark gestured to Jan to take the lead, then followed her along a gloomy corridor towards the back of the house.

Various pieces of stage equipment had been stacked against one wall forming an honour guard of amplifiers, speaker cabinets and guitar cases.

He was taken aback when he stepped into the kitchen.

A light, airy space, green plants sat in pots along the windowsill and sunlight shone through a skylight set into the ceiling.

Nothing like the drab and dirty area he'd been half-expecting.

Toby noticed his surprise, and smiled. 'My girlfriend's the one with green fingers, not me. Do you want a cuppa?'

'No, that's fine, thanks. Mind if we ask you some questions?'

'Sure. This about the old priest that was murdered over at Upper Benham?'

'That's right. Did you know him?'

The guitarist shook his head. 'Never met him. Bit of a shock, though finding out he'd been killed while we were playing. Is that why no-one found him until the morning?'

Mark managed a smile. 'I don't think your playing was to blame. From what we understand, all services had finished for the night and he was about to lock up.'

Toby's shoulders relaxed a little. 'What do you need to speak to me for, then?'

'Routine enquiries. Did you notice anything unusual when you were packing up after your gig?'

'No – it was pretty late by then, and I was keen to get home. I'd played five gigs in a row, and Dean had already headed off. All of the PA kit is mine, so once he'd helped me get it out to the car park, he left me to it.'

'Seems a bit mean,' said Jan.

Toby gave a wry smile. 'That's Dean. Thinks he's a rock star, and I'm his roadie.'

'How long have you been playing?' said Mark.

'Since I was fourteen. My dad used to play in a covers band when I was growing up, so I guess it was inevitable. Half the guitars out there in the hallway were his.'

'He doesn't play anymore?'

'No. Died of cancer three years ago.'

'Sorry to hear that.'

Toby shrugged. 'Mum always told him the cigarettes would be the death of him, silly bugger.'

'Did you learn at school?'

'No – Dad taught me, then when I was sixteen I started earning some pocket money and went for lessons with a guy who played in a rock and blues outfit. That's more what I was interested in. The covers band stuff pays the rent.'

'That's the one you're in with Dean?'

'Yeah.'

'How long have you known him?'

Toby exhaled and gazed at the ceiling. 'Must be going on four years now. Yeah. About that. He moved from Bristol – or somewhere near there. Can't remember the name of the place.'

'Like I said, we got your phone number from Terry Benedict but we'd like to talk to Dean as well. Do you know where we'd find him?'

'He lives over at Radley.'

'Got a phone number?'

'Sure. Hang on.'

They waited while he fished out a mobile phone from his back pocket and scrolled through the contacts.

'Here you go.'

Jan copied down the phone number and an address. 'Does he own the property?'

Toby guffawed. 'Come off it. We don't earn that much. He rents – mind you, his mum and dad own the house, so it's not like it costs him much anyway.'

'Do you socialise much outside of working together?'

'Not really. He'd drive me up the wall, to be honest.'

'Oh? Why's that?'

'It's like I said – he's got his sights on bigger things. Thinks the covers band is beneath him, but like me he needs the money to pay the rent.'

'What about you? What do you want to do with your music?'

He smiled. 'I'm already living the dream. I got picked up by a producer in Manchester four months ago who's working with the "next big thing",' he said, accentuating the words with his fingers. 'I'll be touring with her from October. That's why all the kit's out in the hallway. I'm heading back there at the weekend for a recording session after doing a gig in Birmingham. Rumour has it she's in with a chance of this year's Christmas number one.'

Mark frowned. 'I didn't think there was much call for guitarists these days. Thought it was all that electronic stuff.'

'Ah, you'd be surprised. I might get pushed back into the mix, but it's a layer they want to have to her songs, so I'm not complaining.'

'We'll need a note of where you'll be staying, in case we have further questions,' said Jan.

'Thought you might. Got your pen handy?'

Mark waited while he gave an address to Jan to write down, and then cleared his throat. 'Any idea where Dean might be today?'

'Probably at home. We did a gig last night, and he doesn't tend to do much the day after. Says it's because he has to take care of his voice.'

He led them back to the front door, and Mark waited until he'd stepped over the threshold before turning back to Toby and putting his hand in his pocket.

'Terry Benedict asked me to pass these on. Apparently, they were dropped at your gig in the White Horse the other night.'

Toby held out his hand, and then laughed. 'They're not mine – they're Dean's.'

'How can you tell?'

'He only plays a bit of guitar, but he insists on having these custom-made plectrums. See this lion engraved on the back? They cost a fortune.'

'You don't use these yourself?'

He grinned. 'No, they're crap. He only poses with the guitar so it doesn't make a lot of difference to him.'

'I heard he trained in a choir while he was living near Bristol. Any idea why he left?'

A cloud crossed the guitarist's features, and he shook his head.

'No. He never talks about his time there.'

CHAPTER TWENTY-SEVEN

The next morning, Mark peered through the windscreen at the tidy bungalow at the end of the cul-de-sac, and checked the address in Jan's notebook.

'This is the one.'

She pulled up to the kerb while he took in the neat lawn and flowerbeds beyond a low brick wall.

'I didn't get the impression that our singer was a keen gardener,' he said.

'If the place belongs to his parents, then I'm sure he's not,' said Jan. 'Maybe they take care of the place.'

Mark dialled the number Toby had given them, but it went to voicemail once more. Having left a message for Dean upon leaving the guitarist's house the previous day that hadn't received a response, he hung up.

'Still no answer. Let's see if anyone is in.'

He led the way through one of two metal gates that separated a concrete driveway from the pavement, noting that net curtains covered the windows. He rapped his knuckles on the front door and rang the doorbell, then turned to Jan.

She was standing at the corner of the house, peering down the side of the building towards a single garage they had spotted from the street. She met his gaze and shook her head.

Mark crouched down and flipped open the letterbox.

A bright hallway led to three open doors but the interior remained silent.

'Hello? Anyone home?'

He dropped the metal flap, and turned away.

'He's either out, or asleep,' he said to Jan as she fell into step beside him and closed the gate.

He paused on the pavement and glanced up and down the street, but there were no pedestrians and the neighbouring properties appeared quiet.

'What you want to do?' said Jan.

He checked his watch. 'It's still early, and the afternoon briefing won't be for a few hours yet. Let's head over to Philip Baxter's church at St Martin's Meadow. I wouldn't mind getting my bearings in relation to his house.'

'Sounds good.'

AN HOUR LATER, Mark shoved his hand in his pockets and cast his gaze along the street before leading the way over the road. He whistled under his breath.

'Now, that's what I call a church,' he said.

Jan gave him a sideways glance. 'What do you mean?'

'Well, look at it – it's even got a proper spire.'

She rolled her eyes. 'You do realise the original Catholic church here was destroyed during the Reformation?'

Mark shrugged. 'It's better than the nineteenth-century monstrosity Seamus Carter presided over. What on earth were the Victorians thinking in Upper Benham?' He didn't wait for her answer and held open the gate in the low wall for her. 'How come this one looks like a proper church?'

Jan shoved her sunglasses onto her head, the sunlight now blocked by horse chestnut trees that created a natural canopy above their heads as they followed a gravel path to the porch.

She paused in her tracks and stooped to read a gravestone. 'The population in a lot of these villages was decimated during the First World War, so back in the 1920s this one was handed over to the Catholic Church from the Church of England. They had more parishioners in the neighbouring village and decided to combine the two congregations rather than have the expense of a priest in each parish. It worked for the Catholic Church's purposes, too.'

Mark exhaled as his eyes took in the rows of stones. 'It's a wonder either of the communities survived, isn't it?'

Jan straightened, and gestured at the church. 'Looks like someone is here.'

Mark turned his attention to where she pointed and noticed a bright-red plastic crate propping open the front door.

'Let's go and have a word, shall we?' he said.

As they drew closer, the inner door opened and a bald man squinted in the bright sunshine as his eyes adjusted from the dim interior, and then blinked at the sight of Mark and Jan advancing towards him.

'Oh, hello,' he said. 'Come for a visit, have we?'

Mark realised the man might assume he and Jan were scouting for something like a christening or wedding venue, and quickly retrieved his warrant card from his pocket to avoid any embarrassment.

'A visit of sorts,' he said. 'And you are?'

'Father Templeton. Are you the ones investigating Philip's murder?'

'We are, yes. Mind if we have a word?'

Templeton's shoulders heaved as he gave a huge

sigh, and, in that moment, Mark heard the weariness escape the priest's calm demeanour.

'Come inside,' said Templeton. He bent down to pick up the red crate before his face twisted in pain.

'Can I take that for you?' said Mark.

'Would you mind? I hurt my back pruning the brambles behind the church at the weekend, and I don't like to take too many painkillers. You never know what's in them these days.'

Mark cradled the crate in his hands, peered at the contents, and then smiled. 'A Frederick Forsyth fan, eh?'

Templeton gestured to Jan to go through the door he held open, then waited until Mark had stepped over the threshold.

'Oh, yes,' he said. 'Anything like that. And Alistair Maclean. We're organising a book sale to raise some money for a commemorative plaque in Father Baxter's memory, so I thought I'd pass them along. Every penny helps, after all.'

He directed them across to a growing pile of books and bric-à-brac behind the back pews, then gestured to the empty seats. 'Thank you. Now, what can I do for you?'

Mark waited until Jan had settled and was poised with pen and notebook ready, then turned his attention back to Templeton.

'Did Philip Baxter seem at all troubled in the past few weeks? Did he seem worried about anything?'

Templeton pursed his lips and leaned against the hard wooden surface. He frowned.

'Not overly so, I'd say. I mean, we all have our concerns, and from time to time a particular member of our community might be going through a bad patch, or we might be having difficulties with finances from time to time, but nothing more untoward than that.'

'Business as usual, then?'

That raised a rueful smile.

'Yes,' said Templeton. 'Business as usual.'

'So, Father Baxter made no mention to you of anyone threatening him, or causing him distress?'

Templeton's smile faded, and he reached forward to trace his fingers over an embossed symbol of the cross on the cover of the Bible in the pew before him.

'Now why would you ask that?' he said.

Mark's heart skipped a beat. 'Did something happen? When?'

Templeton closed his eyes a moment. 'Two weeks ago – I can't remember if it was the Tuesday or the Thursday Mass – a man appeared at the doorway halfway through the service, and sat where you are now.' He gave a shudder and opened his eyes. 'I only saw him because Philip had asked me to give the reading. Otherwise, I'd have been sat off to the side, and my view would have been blocked by the congregation.'

'Did you recognise him?'

'No, but that's the thing. When he approached the altar to take the sacrament with everyone else, Philip saw him and nearly dropped the chalice. I thought he was going to, to be honest. When he gave the man the sacrament, his hands were shaking. Afterwards, we were standing thanking everyone for coming along and just general chitchat when the man approached Philip and asked to have a word with him in private. Philip looked scared stiff.'

'What did he do?'

'He is – was – a priest. He couldn't refuse if someone wanted to undertake the sacrament of reconciliation.'

'Reconciliation?' said Mark.

Templeton gave him a sad smile. 'Confession. One of the hardest burdens to bear.'

'You don't know what was said? Philip didn't tell you?'

'It would defeat the object of the exercise, wouldn't it, detective?'

'What happened when the man left?'

'Oh, Philip tried to laugh it off, but I could see he was upset.'

'Did he tell you the man's name?'

'No – he didn't want to talk about it. Kept changing the subject. I could take a hint, so I stopped asking.'

'Have you seen the man since?'

'No.'

'Would you be able to describe him if I got a sketch artist over to you?'

'Well – I don't know. Do you think it would help?'

'Father Templeton, I'll be honest with you. I don't know, but right now you're one of the few good leads I've got.'

'In that case, I'll do my best. Goodness knows what we're going to do here without Philip. He was like a brother to me.'

Tears welled in his eyes, and Mark reached out and squeezed the man's shoulder.

'We'll be in touch.'

CHAPTER TWENTY-EIGHT

Mark let the cooling first taste of the local ale slip down his throat, placed the pint glass on the table in front of him and sighed as he leaned back and turned his gaze to the passing pedestrians on the concrete wharf beyond the window.

The pub was quiet, with only a murmur of voices from two men sitting on stools beside the bar, conversing with the landlord, Gary, about the latest football score.

The regulars had given him a cursory glance as he'd entered, recognising him as some form of authority, but had lost interest when Gary poured his drink without waiting to be asked, evidently sensing he was a known quantity and not interested in them.

The clang and clatter of pans behind the door to his rear announced the kitchen staff preparing for that evening's food orders, and Mark's stomach rumbled in response.

He picked up the motorbike magazine he'd bought on the way home, flicked to the next page with mild irritation at the number of advertisements he had to endure to find something worth reading, then gave up and reached over to the table beside him for the national newspaper a previous patron had left behind.

Gary wandered over to collect an empty pint glass and crisp packet from a neighbouring table and peered over his glasses at Mark as he wiped the pockmarked surface.

'Bad day?'

Mark grimaced and flattened the creases out of the newspaper, turning the front page. 'Frustrating.'

Gary grunted in response, then returned to the bar as the door opened and a young couple hurried in, full of laughter and loud conversation.

Mark yawned, his eyes scanning the newsprint as he took another sip from his drink. His phone vibrated in his pocket and he felt the familiar adrenalin spike of worry from being submerged within an ongoing murder investigation.

Retrieving it, his panic changed tone as he recognised Debbie's number.

'Everything all right?'

'Hello to you, too.'

'Are the girls okay?'

'They're fine.'

He relaxed his grip on the phone. 'You had me worried for a moment there.'

'You're back at work, aren't you?'

'How did you—'

'You always imagine the worst when you're working. I thought you had another couple of weeks before you were due to start?'

'Something came up.'

'Oh.'

He could hear realisation dawn on her.

'The murdered priests? You're involved?'

'Yes.' He sipped his drink. 'Got pulled in early.'

'You okay with that?'

'I didn't have a lot of choice.'

'No, I suppose not.'

He switched the phone to his other hand and leaned back against his chair, his gaze turning to the river.

A cruiser eased along the current, its occupants waving to two fishermen on the quay as they passed. Two women sat on the sofas at the bow, champagne flutes in hand, while the man steering adjusted his baseball cap and concentrated on preparing to pass under the bridge.

'Everything okay?' Debbie's voice pulled him back to the pub.

'Watching boats on the river.'

'As if you're not getting enough of boats already.' Her words were kind, not accusatory. 'Have you managed to find anywhere more permanent to live?'

'Not yet. I don't think the girls will complain. They loved it here the other weekend.'

'I know – they wouldn't stop talking about it.'

They both laughed.

'What did you want me for?' he said, then stuck up his thumb as Gary wandered over and gestured at his empty glass. He placed his hand over the microphone. 'Thanks.'

The landlord winked, and retreated.

'Thought you might like to know that Anna did well in her English test last week. She got the results this morning.'

'Oh, that's fantastic. Is she not there at the moment?'

'Girl Guides tonight, otherwise she'd tell you herself. They've got camp for a week in August so I've got to head off in a while to pick her up and get my marching orders for that. No doubt it'll be bedlam.'

'No doubt. At least you'll have a week's peace and quiet.'

'Have you bumped into Gillian yet?' she said, her voice feigning innocence.

He managed a chuckle. 'No doubt you've heard all about it. She's never going to forgive me, is she?'

Debbie sighed. 'It's only because our parents split up when we were young, you know that. I suppose given that she and Alistair don't have any kids, she worries about the effect all of this will have on the girls. I've told her it's not your fault – it's the job. Give her a chance.'

'That works both ways, Debs.'

They spoke for another five minutes, and then her voice grew serious.

'Are you okay, Mark? You're not simply saying that?'

'I'm okay. Promise. Will you give my love to Anna and Louise, and tell Anna well done on those results for me?'

'Will do.'

She ended the call, and he glanced up in time to see Gary advancing towards him with a full glass.

'Thanks for that.'

'You eating tonight?'

'No, I'm fine, thanks.'

He waited until Gary moved away, and then turned his attention back to the newspaper, glass in hand.

Truth be told, he was starving, but what with the prospect of buying a car and the cost of renting the boat and saving for a house, he was starting to feel the pinch. It'd be beans on toast tonight, and nothing more extravagant for a while.

He blinked, a sense of unease clutching at his mind.

He pushed the drink to one side, and raised the paper to read more closely, the noise around him fading to a distant murmur as the words sank in.

A priest had been arrested in Australia for historic abuse, and the paper had reprinted an opinion piece by a journalist based in Melbourne.

The reporter had been careful in her coverage of the story – to her credit, it wasn't sensationalist or accusatory but expressed sadness that such crimes continued to be covered up by the Church. The reportage included a call for the country's authorities to do more to protect those who had been affected and charge the men responsible. It ended with a demand for the silence to stop, for the church to formally recognise that it had been at fault, and to provide compensation to the victims involved.

Mark raised his head and stared at the opposite wall, his heart racing.

He eyed the half-finished ale, then pushed back his chair and grabbed the newspaper, sweeping his jacket over his shoulders. Flinging the door open, he called over his shoulder.

'I'll square up with you tomorrow, Gary. Got to go.'

He nearly collided with an elderly man on the pavement as he rounded the corner, and, after apologising profusely and ensuring no harm had been done, he set off once more, his mind racing as fast as his footsteps.

By the time he reached the police station, sweat was pouring down his brow and between his shoulders.

He ignored the shocked expression on Sergeant Wilcox's face, and took the stairs two at a time to the second floor, then raced along the corridor to the incident room.

DI Kennedy glanced up from a report he was reading as Mark burst into his office, panting.

'What on earth—'

Mark leaned forwards and placed one hand on his knee, raising the other to silence the DI. 'Give me a second, guv.'

Once he'd got his breath back, he straightened to see Kennedy's expression turn from surprise to concern.

'Are you all right?' He raised himself from his chair. 'Do you want a glass of water?'

Mark waved him back into his seat. 'I'm fine. Just more out of shape than I thought.'

The DI's brow puckered, but he sat down. 'I take it you want to speak to me?'

Mark nodded, inhaled another lungful of air, then collapsed into a seat opposite.

'What if this isn't about what those priests might have done to someone?'

'What do you mean?'

Mark slapped the newspaper onto the desk, flicked through the pages until he found the article, then spun it around and stabbed his finger on the headline. 'What if this is about ensuring their silence, or revenge against those who might've been abusers?'

He watched as the DI's gaze flickered over the words before he raised his eyes to Mark's and stabbed his finger at the middle of the page.

'Explain.'

'What if both Seamus Carter and Philip Baxter knew something and helped to cover it up? What if their killer has had some sort of complaint against the church? If it hasn't been taken seriously, he could've decided to take matters into his own hands.'

Kennedy pushed his chair back and shoved his hands in his pockets as he stalked over to the window. 'It'd certainly give our killer a motive, either way.'

'Exactly. I think we should speak to Jan's contact at the diocesan office again and find out if there were any complaints made by – or against – our two victims. At least then we'll be able to establish a pool of potential suspects with better clarity.'

The DI turned back to the room. 'Make it a priority. I'll update the team with your theory at the briefing tomorrow morning.'

Mark nodded. 'Thanks, guv.'

'In the meantime, you look like you're about to have a heart attack. Go home and get some rest, for goodness' sakes.'

CHAPTER TWENTY-NINE

Robert Argyle glanced up at the darkening sky, leaned the garden fork against the weather-beaten wooden shed and stretched his back muscles.

The clay soil clung to the soles of his Wellington boots and made tending the vegetable patch hard work, but he relished being outside and seeing the fruits of his labour grow under his care.

The runner beans stretched above him, winding their way up the bamboo poles he'd strung together one morning in late March, and he reckoned he'd have a bumper harvest by summer.

Next to where he stood, carrot tops poked through the dirt, and he placed a length of netting across the infant crop, driving stakes into the ground to stop the local rabbit population from helping themselves to his food.

The forecast rain shower would save him spending the next half an hour standing over the garden with a hose pipe, and as he walked down the garden path towards the back door of the cottage, his mouth watered at the thought of the cold beer in the refrigerator.

He stopped at the threshold, scraped off the worst of the mud from his boots, and then sat on a rubber door mat covering the kitchen step to slip them off. Propping them up in a corner next to the washing machine inside the door, he rested his forearms on his knees and took a moment to savour the colours that washed the sky in hues of gold, orange and purple.

After a few moments of quiet reflection, he stood and closed the door, flicked the switch for the spotlights in the ceiling, and then reached up and slid the bolt across the doorframe.

It gleamed in the light reflected from above, its shiny surface free from grease.

Robert's mouth thinned.

He'd purchased it on Monday, hurrying through the doors of the cavernous hardware store as soon as they were opened, not wishing to waste time.

His purchases had used up most of his weekly shopping budget, but he didn't care.

By the time he'd finished, the bolt was secured to the back door, a new lock had been fitted to the front entrance together with a chain, and he'd drilled a locking bolt into the window track of the patio doors at the rear of the property for good measure. His work was complete once each of the downstairs windows had been fitted with a lock as well, and he kept the keys on a chain fixed to his belt.

He wasn't taking any chances.

He released a shaking breath, then set his shoulders and peeled off his sweatshirt and hung it over the back of one of three chairs at a dining table, then opened the refrigerator.

Three tall bottles of real ale stood on the middle shelf and as he grasped the one on the right, his thumb slid down the condensation and he wet his lips in anticipation.

He pulled a pint glass from a cupboard above the microwave, and tried to ignore his trembling hands as he poured the beer.

Placing the empty bottle next to the sink, he padded through to the living room, then loosened the white collar at his neck, dropped it onto the coffee table and sank into one of two armchairs that faced a television.

He didn't switch it on.

He didn't need to see the pain and suffering broadcast from all around the world to his living room.

Robert tipped back the glass and swallowed a quarter of the drink in two gulps.

It did nothing to soothe his frayed nerves as the memories resurfaced.

Of all the burdens of his role as a priest in the Roman Catholic Church, the sacrament of reconciliation was the hardest to bear.

Over the years, he had heard them all – the petty theft, the adultery, the envy that had driven normal people to sinful acts.

However, there was one that stood out and sent a chill coursing down his spine.

The memory had never left him. It would fade, over time, and then the simplest of tasks would cause him to remember and leave him with nightmares for weeks as he wrestled with his conscience.

The voice that had murmured to him through the wall of the confessional had been matter-of-fact, as if discussing a leaking tap that had been fixed.

His mind had raced as it processed the words, shock turning to horror, and then fear. His own voice had shaken as he'd prescribed the penance – and then, as now, he felt repulsed at his attempts to excuse the sin that had been committed.

The voice on the other side of the screen had mumbled the act of contrition before movement reached his ears, and he realised the man had left the confessional, footsteps fading on the flagstone floor as he hurried from the church.

Afterwards, he had hidden in the vestry with a bottle of whisky he kept locked in the bottom drawer of his desk.

He had wrestled with his conscience over the years, of course, but the problem was that his belief in the Seal of the Confessional prevented him from telling anyone else about what he had heard. Under the law of the church, if he did so, he would be automatically punished with excommunication.

His life as he knew it would be over. He would no longer be at one with his God.

He exhaled, a ragged breath that shuddered from his lungs and left him fearful for his sanity.

He knew he should tell someone – but who?

The bishop was miles away, and any request for an audience would be met with first disbelief, and then at least a two-week waiting period.

The police were out of the question, for how could he explain?

It wasn't as if he could retract his statement if his conscience suddenly reminded him of his duty halfway through speaking to one of them. He'd seen the press conference on Saturday, and noted the determination in the faces of the detectives who faced the glare from the media's cameras, their voices clear and steady as they gave details of their investigation and called for calm – as well as help.

He took another sip of beer and then ran a hand across tired eyes.

He would finish his drink, and then pray. Pray for guidance, for forgiveness, for hope.

For he had nothing else to hold on to.

A thump on the carpet above shook him from his thoughts, and his gut twisted painfully.

He held his breath as his eyes traced the whorls in the ceiling, his mouth open.

Silently, he reached out and placed the pint glass on the table and leaned forward, his senses alert.

He forced himself to sit still, straining his ears for any sound, willing his heart rate to slow so it wouldn't rush in his ears and obscure his hearing. He was panting now, the ancient instinct of fight or flight causing his chest to tighten.

And then he heard it.

A *creak* from behind him as the door through to the hallway was pushed open.

Horror gripped him as he realised all his efforts to protect himself had been in vain.

There was someone else in the house.

CHAPTER THIRTY

'We need to stop meeting like this.'

'Tell me about it.' Jan floored the accelerator the moment Turpin slammed the car door shut.

'What time is it anyway?' he said, yawning noisily as he leaned forward and tied his shoelaces.

'Quarter to midnight. Wake you, did I?'

'I needed an early night.'

She bit back a smile at his defensive tone. A curse emanated from the opposite side of the car and she glanced across. 'You all right?'

'Trod in mud crossing the meadow. Jesus.'

'Back seat. There's an old towel Scott keeps there for after he plays football. Use that.'

'Thanks.'

They fell silent, the road twisting and turning as they passed through sleepy villages, Jan taking full advantage of the quiet roads to reach their destination as fast as possible.

'Whereabouts are we going?'

'Malden Cross. It's another two miles.'

'What do you know so far?'

'Like I said on the phone, another priest attacked at home. No news yet on whether he's dead or alive.' She slapped the wheel. 'And we're no closer to finding out who's doing this.'

'I spoke with the DI earlier.'

Jan listened as Turpin explained his theory, then nodded. 'It's a sound one. I'll get onto the diocesan office in the morning. There has to be something there we're missing.'

She braked heavily, then took a sharp left-hand turning into a narrow lane bordered by tall hedgerows on either side. Gritting her teeth as a rabbit shot across the pockmarked asphalt in front of them, she eyed the speedometer and lifted her foot off the pedal a little.

'Nearly there,' she muttered.

'What's the address?'

She rattled it off from memory and a glow illuminated Turpin's features as he used his phone to find the exact location of the crime scene moments before he began to recite directions.

The sign for Malden Cross flashed past on Jan's

left, and then she took a right-hand turn after a barn conversion and gasped, hitting the brakes hard.

Turpin gritted his teeth as his seatbelt pressed into his chest, then swore when he peered through the windscreen.

'Shit.'

The media had beaten them to it this time, and a young uniformed officer who looked as if she'd only recently left training college was doing her best to keep a cordon between the throng and the crime scene.

Jan applied the handbrake and hurried towards the cottage, Turpin close behind.

A commotion near the front door caused a flurry of activity amongst the journalists that stood next to the tape marking the boundary to the crime scene, and a shout reached her as she realised a pair of paramedics were wheeling a stretcher out of the house towards a waiting ambulance.

'He's alive,' she said.

Turpin pushed past her, headed towards the female officer and helped her to push the onlookers out of the way, removing his jacket and holding it above the victim's face to shield him from the flurry of flashlights from both press photographers' cameras and neighbours using smartphones.

As she caught up with him, Jan heard him curse under his breath. A microphone was thrust under his nose, and she raised her hand to ward off any further comment, glaring at the culprit.

Four uniformed officers joined them and, between them, they raised blankets to shield the stretcher from further intrusion as it was loaded into the back of the ambulance.

Finally, the paramedics jumped into the vehicle and it tore away, blue lights flashing.

Turpin gestured towards the cottage and then shrugged his jacket over his shoulders. 'Shall we?'

She fell into step beside him, dropping the tape into place while she ignored the shouted questions and grumbles from the crowd. Her focus turned to the uniformed sergeant who took a clipboard from PC Willis on the doorstep and thrust it towards her.

'The crime scene investigators got here fifteen minutes ago,' he said. 'From what I gather, there's no sign of a break-in and it appears that his attacker was lying in wait.'

'You were able to talk with the victim?' said Jan.

He nodded. 'One of the neighbours heard a scuffle and called in. We happened to be passing on a routine patrol, so we were here within ten minutes of the shout.' He jerked his chin in the direction the ambulance had taken. 'His name's Robert Argyle. Parish priest for Malden Cross and two of the neighbouring hamlets.'

'What are his injuries?' said Turpin, craning his neck to see around Willis.

'Significant bruising to his neck – his voice is damaged from it – but he told us his attacker had tried to strangle him with a rope. He's missing part of his ear as well.'

Turpin's hand moved to his throat as the police constable continued.

'He somehow landed a punch, and that's when his assailant took off. Argyle managed to dial triple nine but of course we were already on our way by then.'

'Any sign of the attacker?' said Jan.

'The kitchen door had been left open, but we haven't managed to find any fingerprints. We've done a preliminary search of the back garden – now that the CSIs are here, we'll do it again with the aid of their floodlights. There are three patrols out around the village checking exit roads and I've this moment finished organising house-to-house enquiries.' His top lip curled as his gaze lifted to the cordon beyond the gate. 'If half of them spent as much attention to anything going on outside as they are filming what's going on here, we might find something of use.'

Jan shared his sentiment about the neighbours, but any response was cut short by a shout from the side of the cottage.

'Sarge?'

She recognised Peter Cosley from the station as he emerged from the side of the house, beckoning them closer to the taped perimeter.

'What have you got?'

Turpin beat her by a footstep, and she joined him, slightly out of breath from the adrenalin that spiked her heart rate.

'What is it, Cosley?' she said.

In reply, the bespectacled police sergeant held up a small plastic object that he'd bagged and sealed.

Jan peered closer, and frowned.

'A guitar plectrum?'

'Found it on the path leading from the back door. There's a gate that leads to a track going down to the stream.'

'Footprints?' said Turpin.

'A few. We're in the process of taking casts. Seems to be a popular route for dog walkers, given the number of paw prints.'

'Can I take a closer look?'

The constable handed the plectrum to Jan, who turned it in her hands. After a moment, she lifted her gaze to Turpin and grinned.

'It's got a lion on the back, see?'

'The same as Toby said Dean Harper uses?'

'Where exactly was this found?' said Jan.

'Next to the gate post for the victim's house, where the footpath starts.'

'All right. Thanks,' said Turpin.

They watched as the uniformed officer retreated to the back of the house to join his colleagues once more.

'Do we know if our priest played guitar?'

'Not yet,' said Jan.

'In that case, get onto the control room. I want Dean Harper in custody by the time we get back to the station.'

CHAPTER THIRTY-ONE

Mark waited while Jan recited the formal caution after
he'd switched on the machine beside him, and used the
time to study the twenty-eight-year-old man opposite.

He ignored the duty solicitor – the man was there
to do a job, that was all, despite the expensive-looking
suit and swept-back dyed blond hair.

No, he was interested in watching Dean Harper
absorb the reality that he was in police custody, and
wondered why on earth someone with his obvious
intelligence would kill two men and attempt to murder
a third.

'According to your band's website, you were
brought up in Somerset, educated near Bristol, and
moved to Oxfordshire in 2016,' said Jan. 'You began
your singing career as a choirboy. Tell us about your
time in the parish north of Bristol.'

Dean folded his arms across his chest and jutted out his chin. 'Like what?'

'Like, how did you end up there for a start?'

'Bad luck.' He sighed and dropped his hands into his lap. 'My mum wanted me to be a choirboy. She was really into her religion, y'know? I think she saw it as a way of keeping me out of trouble. We weren't the sort of family who could afford a lot, so I guess that was her way of getting around it.'

'Is that how you got into your music?'

'Yes. I realised I enjoyed the performance part of it, more than anything else. Practising could be boring, especially if some of the younger boys kept forgetting their places, but I loved being on a stage, I guess.'

'When did it start to go wrong?' said Mark.

'What do you mean?'

'We've spoken to the administrative officer for the choir from when you were there. He said that you left when you were fourteen. Why?'

'I got bored I guess.'

'Guess again. Someone like you? You said it yourself – you loved the attention you got when you were singing in front of a congregation. So, why quit?'

He watched as the singer's Adam's apple bobbed in his throat.

'I don't know what you're talking about,' he said finally, his voice hoarse.

Mark leaned forward and rested his arms on the table. 'Oh, I think you do.'

'Do you recognise this?' Jan shoved a plastic bag containing the lion-emblazoned plectrum towards Dean, whose eyes opened wide.

'Where did you get that?'

'Answer the question, please.'

'It's mine. I mean – it looks like one of mine.'

'Which music shop do you buy them from?'

'I-I don't. A mate of mine owns an online store, and I get them custom-made.'

'Care to tell us what it was doing in the grass near Father Robert Argyle's house?'

'Who?'

'Robert Argyle, parish priest for Malden Cross.'

'I've never heard of him.' His eyes flashed between Jan and Mark. 'I have no idea – I'm telling you the truth!'

'Tell us about Father Philip Baxter,' said Mark. 'What did he do to you, Dean? Why did you murder him?'

'I never murdered nobody. What's going on?'

'Father Seamus Carter was murdered the night you played a gig at the White Horse.' Mark flipped open the manila folder at his elbow and shoved a series of photographs across the table.

Both Dean and his duty solicitor recoiled.

'Not a pretty sight, is it?' said Mark. 'Care to tell me what you did with his tongue?'

'W-what?' The singer paled, and for a split second Mark thought he was going to be sick.

'His tongue was cut out while he was still alive, Dean. It was taken. Where did you put it?'

'Jesus Christ, I didn't kill him!'

'What about Philip Baxter? Why did you cut out his eyes? Where are you keeping those, Dean?'

'I've never heard of the man.'

'Where were you on the night of the fifteenth?' said Jan.

'Away.'

'Where?'

Dean shuffled in his seat. 'I met up with some girl I'd seen hanging around a few of our gigs, all right? We bumped into each other at a pub in Oxford. There was a punk band playing. Afterwards, she invited me back to hers.'

'We'll need a name and an address.'

'It was her sister's place. She was only visiting.'

Jan glared at him and shoved a pen and paper across the table. 'Name and address. Now.'

Mark contemplated the younger man while he scrawled across the page with a shaking hand, and narrowed his eyes. 'You're keeping something from us, Dean. If you didn't murder two priests and attack a third, then we need your help – and we need it now. You were a choirboy in that parish. Robert Argyle was a priest there, too. Did something happen? Is that why you're hiding something?

In response, Dean shook his head.

'Dean, please. Jan's going to check out your alibi for that night, but there are two priests lying in a morgue, and one in a hospital, lucky to be alive. You know something, and you need to tell us.'

The singer placed his hands on the table, and then raised his face to the ceiling and closed his eyes.

Moments later, a single tear spilled over his cheek.

'We were told never to speak of it,' he said, his voice barely above a whisper.

Mark held his breath, thankful that Jan remained silent, and waited for him to continue.

'There was a boy, maybe six months older than me,' said Dean. He dropped his chin, and then raised his gaze to meet Mark's, his cheeks flushing. 'It was when I was twelve. That's when I discovered that the priest that taught us choir practice liked his boys.'

Mark held up his hand. 'Were you abused?'

Dean shook his head. 'No. I don't know why. Maybe the dirty old man realised I'd put up a fight, or talk. So, he picked the one who was too scared to say boo to a goose, let alone stand up to a priest and report him.'

'Who?'

'Jeremy Wallace.' Dean snorted. 'He was only a small lad. For his age, I mean. Do you know what I mean if I said he looked delicate?'

Mark nodded, and gestured for him to continue.

'Well, I guess our choir master took a fancy to him.'

'How long did this go on for?'

'Too long. I don't know. He told me about a week before it happened.'

'What happened?' said Jan.

'He killed himself. Couldn't take it anymore. Too embarrassed and scared to talk to his dad. He had no-one. We all turned up one Sunday morning for Mass as usual and he was swinging from a noose in one of the oak trees at the side of the church car park. I'd never seen a dead body before.' Tears streamed down his face, dripping from his jawline as he forced a bitter smile. 'He'd even used one of the dirty bastard's stoles to hang himself, like it was a final defiant gesture.'

Dean pushed the chair back and crossed to the other side of the room, turning his back on them. The sound of his sobbing filled the enclosed space as he hugged his arms around himself.

Mark put his hand on Jan's arm to stop her following, and when she spun on her chair to face him, he shook his head.

'Let him have a moment.'

After a few minutes, Dean squared his shoulders, turned and attempted to compose himself as he returned to the table and slumped in his chair.

Mark plucked two paper tissues from a box beside him and handed them over.

'Thanks.'

'Why did you wait for nearly two years until leaving the choir?'

'I was scared, wasn't I? As it was, I only managed to leave when I got a paper round – I persuaded my mum that would keep me out of trouble, and she could see I was better off earning some money of my own, so she let me quit.'

'Do you know if Jeremy told anyone else about the abuse?'

'I don't know.'

'It wasn't discussed amongst the other choirboys? You didn't overhear the other priests talking to anyone about it?'

'That was the point,' said Dean, wiping angrily at his eyes. 'No-one let on that they heard or saw anything.'

CHAPTER THIRTY-TWO

Mark swore loudly at the sight of two vans emblazoned with local television news logos parked at the kerb outside the police headquarters the following morning, and then changed down a gear and zipped his mountain bike behind a patrol car before the barrier began to close.

Braking next to the entrance into the police station, he removed his helmet and glanced back at the assembled throng.

A male reporter was speaking to the camera, but then turned to another man next to him.

Mark realised it was Gerald Aitchison.

'What are you up to?' he murmured.

He placed the bike in a rack off to one side, then pushed through the door and hurried towards the men's changing rooms. Fifteen minutes later, cycling kit exchanged for his suit and his backpack slung over his shoulder, he hurried into the incident room.

Jan rose from her desk as he approached.

'Did you see Aitchison?'

'Yes. What's he up to?'

'Causing problems, according to the DI. Apparently, he's gone on live television complaining we're not doing enough to catch the killer.' She lowered her voice. 'He's only gone and bloody told them Seamus had his tongue cut out.'

'What?' He glanced over his shoulder to Kennedy's office, and noted the door was closed. 'Who's in with him?'

'Andrew Tolley, head of the media relations team. You can imagine the mood he's in.'

'I don't blame him – how on earth did Aitchison find out about that?'

'No idea.'

'Me neither.' Mark moved to the window and peered out between the slats of the blinds, noting that the councillor had been joined by an entourage of middle-aged men and women who stood by his side.

Aitchison gestured to them with a sweep of his hand, and then turned back to the waiting cameras, and Mark realised he had probably rounded up some of his more fervent constituents to add substance to his protests.

At that moment, one of the women brushed past his elbow and jabbed her finger at one of the reporters before Aitchison placed a hand on her arm and made a point of gently steering her towards an older man who hugged her.

Mark turned away from the window with a snort of derision at the obvious manoeuvre to ensure Aitchison appeared sympathetic yet suitably outraged for the cameras.

'Do you know who any of those people are down there with him?' he asked Jan.

She joined him, running her gaze over the onlookers. 'That woman standing behind him—'

'The one that's being hugged?'

'Yes. I recognise her from the locals that were milling about the crime scene at Upper Benham on Sunday morning. I don't think you spotted her because you were looking at Gillian's car. I overheard someone say she works in the village shop. The bloke with her must be her husband.'

'So, it was her assistant I spoke to about the extra keys for the church – Jim Aster.'

'That's the one.'

'What about the others down there?'

She tapped the window. 'The man to Aitchison's

left is Michael Westing. He calls himself a campaign manager. Aitchison brought him in on a consultancy basis when he announced he'd be running in the next by-election. I don't know who any of the others are. Rent-a-mob, by the looks of some of them.'

'They've been interviewed?'

'Uniform took statements after Seamus's murder, yes. The woman, Kath Hamdan, said Seamus had been into the shop on the Friday – she thought he looked concerned about something when he came in apparently, but had laughed it off as nothing serious when she'd asked. Uniform wondered if it was connected, but she then backed down and said she could've been mistaken.'

'And yet she thought to raise it in the first place.' Mark glanced over his shoulder and rubbed his jaw. 'Maybe we should have another word with her, especially since that assistant of hers – Jim – said there wasn't a record of any other keys being cut for the church. Maybe he was mistaken.'

'I'll get her phone number from HOLMES2. What about her husband?'

'What does he do? Do we know?'

'Mechanic for one of the local agriculture machinery firms. He made no mention of speaking with Seamus – just attends the church when his wife insists, apparently.'

'All right. Looks like the party's over down there.' He reached out and grabbed his jacket.

'Where are you going?' said Jan, raising her eyebrows.

'To have a chat with our esteemed local councillor.'

CHAPTER THIRTY-THREE

'Mr Aitchison – a word, if you don't mind.'

Mark stalked across the car park to the locked gates, and noted with satisfaction that the local councillor's head jerked around at the sound of his voice.

His eyes narrowed. 'You missed your opportunity to speak with the press, detective. You should have been here ten minutes ago.' He turned to the man beside him. 'Michael and I were just saying that it would've been prudent to have your side of the story, after all. Sadly, they've departed – no doubt to polish their stories before this evening's news.'

Mark ignored the campaign manager, who held out his hand whilst a sneer peeled back his lips.

'Oh, I don't tend to get involved with the media if I can help it,' he said. 'I'll leave that to my DI and our media liaison officer. I'm sure they'll have something to say about your little publicity stunt.' He pressed the button to release the locking mechanism. 'I would, however, like a word with you. In private.'

He glared at Michael Westing who had taken a step forward, then beckoned to Aitchison. 'Come on. I haven't got all day. You want this murder inquiry solved, then we need to talk.'

The councillor's expression turned from smugness to panic. 'Well, I – is that appropriate? I mean—'

'We can make it a formal interview if you wish. Your choice.'

Aitchison cleared his throat. 'I'm sure that won't be necessary.'

Mark slammed the gate shut and turned his back on Westing, leading the councillor across the car park and into the police station. He didn't break his stride, swiping his security card and leading the way into the custody suite.

An angry shout preceded a loud *clang* from behind one of the doors, and Mark's mouth twitched as Aitchison reared away from the sudden protest with a frightened yelp.

'In here.' He swung open the door to the interview room, waited until Aitchison passed, then slammed it shut with as much force as he could summon.

The councillor spun around, his mouth open in shock.

Mark jabbed his forefinger at the four chairs that surrounded a single table bolted to the floor. 'Sit down.'

Aitchison's Adam's apple bobbed once in his throat, and then he slid onto the nearest chair and tried to look indignant. 'Listen, I don't know—'

Mark perched on the corner of the desk and glowered at him, the man's words falling silent under his gaze. 'How did you know Seamus Carter's tongue was removed?'

Aitchison reached up to straighten his tie, his eyes falling away from Mark's glare and finding a spot on the tiled floor instead. He mumbled.

'I didn't hear that, Gerald. Speak up.'

'I said, I was told.'

'So, you provided a quote to the press based on hearsay? Seems unprofessional for an aspiring politician. Who told you?'

'I can't remember.'

Mark folded his arms across his chest. 'I've got all day to wait until you *do* remember. How do you think your so-called campaign manager out there will field any requests for comment while you're in here? Tell them you're assisting us with our enquiries?'

Aitchison paled. 'You wouldn't dare.'

Mark pushed himself away from the desk, and

walked over to the door. Opening it, he fished his mobile phone from his pocket and dialled Jan's number.

'We're in the middle of the briefing up here,' she hissed. 'Where the hell are you?'

'Meet me in interview room two,' he said. 'I need you to sit in on a formal interview I want to conduct with Gerald Aitchison.'

He ignored the squawk of protest from the councillor behind him and pulled the door shut, pacing the corridor until he heard footsteps.

'What's going on?'

Jan pushed a tendril of hair behind her ear and hurried towards him, a quizzical expression pinching her features.

Mark jerked his thumb over his shoulder. 'I can't make up my mind if he's stupid or actually might know something about Seamus's death, but I want to make it formal before I go any further.'

'Oh. Okay.'

He nodded, thankful she hadn't sought to question him about his reasons, and held open the door for her.

He pulled out a chair opposite Aitchison and sat down, then waited until Jan hit the "record" button on the machine at the far end of the desk and read out the formal caution, noting with some satisfaction that

Aitchison turned a sickly grey as realisation dawned on him that his was a serious predicament.

'Do I need a solicitor?'

'That's up to you,' said Mark. 'You're not under arrest. As my colleague here has explained to you, this is a formal interview. Do you wish a solicitor to be present?'

Aitchison swallowed, appeared to contemplate Mark's words as his gaze found the closed door, and then shook his head.

'No. I've got nothing to hide. I don't need a solicitor.'

'Why are you talking to the press about an ongoing murder investigation, Mr Aitchison?'

'I told you, the whole village is concerned that his killer is still out there. He's killed again, hasn't he? What's to say there won't be more?'

'More?' Mark leaned forward. 'Can you explain that statement, Mr Aitchison? Do you know something I don't?'

Flustered, Aitchison sat back in his seat, his mouth opening and closing but no sound escaping.

'If you're withholding information that could assist this investigation, I suggest you tell me. Now,' said Mark. He leaned forward and folded his hands on the table between them. 'Only a handful of people knew about Seamus's tongue. And that didn't include any members of the public. The only person outside of my colleagues at the crime scene who would have known about the injuries caused to Seamus is his killer. Where were you the night of his death?'

'I beg your pardon?'

'Answer the question, please.'

'I-I was in. At home, I mean.'

'All night?'

'Yes.'

'Can anyone corroborate that?'

Mark relished the panicked expression that flittered across Aitchison's face as the man dropped his gaze to his hands and took a deep breath.

'I have to ask that this is treated with the utmost secrecy,' he said.

'That depends on whether what you tell us has a bearing on our investigation,' said Mark. 'Who can confirm your whereabouts?'

'There's – there's a website, all right? You can go on there and chat with people.'

Mark narrowed his eyes. 'What sort of people?'

'Oh – nothing dodgy.' Aitchison emitted a nervous bark of laughter, then fell silent once more.

'Who were you talking to?'

Aitchison sighed. 'Her name's Amelia. Croatian, I think. Lovely person. Hoping to get a residency visa in the near future.' He held up his hand, his cheeks flushed. 'It's nothing illegal, I promise. Look, since my wife divorced me, I've been lonely. That's all. It helps.'

'We'll need the details of the website, and for Amelia's contact details.'

Aitchison nodded, resigned.

'Philip Baxter.'

'What about him?'

'Did you ever make a phone call to him?'

'No – why would I?'

'Were you aware if any complaints had been made about Seamus Carter?'

'Complaints?'

'Yes. Had any of your constituents ever raised any concerns about Seamus's conduct within the parish?'

Aitchison shook his head. 'No. Nothing like that.'

'Tell me how you knew that Seamus's tongue had been removed.'

'Kath. She owns the local shop and runs the post office. She told me.'

'The woman who was outside with you just now when you were talking to the press?'

'Yes.'

'How did she find out?'

'I don't know. She didn't say.'

'When did she tell you?'

'The Monday afternoon. After he was found.'

'What exactly did she say?'

'I was posting some new campaign leaflets – I wanted to reach some influential people, and they don't take kindly to cold callers on their doorsteps. She served me in the post office as usual, then said had I heard that Seamus had had his tongue removed? I was shocked, to be honest. I mean, you just don't think that sort of thing would happen around here, do you?'

'And you didn't think to tell us?'

'Well, I mean – what was the point? You'd have already known, wouldn't you?'

Mark eyed the man for a moment longer, then sighed. 'If you're so concerned about us finding Seamus Carter's killer, Mr Aitchison, then you have to let us do our jobs. Running off to the press might make you look good and give you your fifteen minutes of fame, but the damage you've caused by passing on information about an ongoing murder investigation is a serious matter.'

Aitchison paled once more. 'I-I didn't mean—'

'Yes, you did. You didn't think of the consequences of your actions at all.' Mark shook his head. 'You've told the press an intimate detail about Seamus's death that only members of this investigation team know about. Have you any idea of the damage you've done by letting the killer know – on national television no less – the angle of our enquiries?'

He reached across to the recording equipment. 'Interview terminated at eight twenty-two.'

'You're letting me go?'

Mark pushed his chair backwards and pointed at the door. 'I told you, you're not under arrest. Yet. However, we'll be referring this matter to our Senior Investigating Officer. He may take a different view, so if I were you I'd phone a solicitor. Get out of my sight, Aitchison.'

Mark paced the interview room as Jan led the chastened councillor out into the corridor and took a moment to calm himself before making his way back through to the reception desk as the back door to the station swung shut.

Jan turned on hearing footsteps, then waited while he joined her at the glass window. 'Do you think he's our killer?'

'No. I think he knows more than he's telling us though.'

Mark watched as Aitchison crossed the car park and slipped through the gap in the fence before the gate had fully opened, hurrying towards Michael Westing, who was standing next to the open door of a russet-coloured car on the opposite side of the road.

The two men conversed briefly before Aitchison strode around to the passenger side and lowered himself into the vehicle. Westing glared at the closed doors to the reception area, then climbed in behind the steering wheel and eased the car away from the kerb.

A sense of unease prickled at Mark's neck as he watched them go.

Eventually, he turned to see Tom Wilcox leaning on the desk, his face inquisitive.

'Think he'll be back, Sarge?'

'I bloody hope not.'

CHAPTER THIRTY-FOUR

Jan squared her shoulders and pushed open the door into the Upper Benham general stores and post office, a brass bell tinkling in its bracket above her head announcing her arrival.

Turpin followed in her wake, content to leave the questioning to her. They'd agreed during the drive over that she would lead the conversation, reasoning that Kath Hamdan would probably respond better being interviewed by another woman.

Turpin planned to hover on the fringes of the shop, within earshot.

The pungent scent of lavender overwhelmed Jan's senses as she ran her gaze over a display of soaps on the shelves to her right amongst the clutter of knick-knacks that she hadn't seen since visiting her grandmother as a child. She wondered if people still bought such things, and turned her attention to the rest of the shop.

To her left, a newspaper rack sat half full with that morning's editions – the usual tabloid dross accompanied by the local offerings side by side with gossip magazines and puzzle books.

A bored-looking teenager peered at her from behind a counter next to the display, a wariness in her pale-blue eyes.

Jan held up her warrant card. 'We were hoping to speak with Kath.'

The girl jerked her head towards the back of the shop. 'Post office.'

'Ta.'

She craned her neck to see over the shelves of long-life milk, biscuits, cleaning products and other stuff the owners had deemed appropriate stock for the inhabitants of the village, then hovered at the end of a short queue of customers lined up in front of the post office counter.

As she waited in line beside Turpin, she took in the pinched expression of the stocky woman behind the glass partition.

Kath Hamdan moved with a practised efficiency, mumbling a half-hearted greeting to each person who approached, and shoving loose change and receipts back through a metal tray as if to send them away as soon as possible.

Then, her eyes met Jan's and an "o" of shock formed on her lips.

She muttered a curt response to the last of her customers, an elderly gentleman who shuffled away from the counter, and then she glared at the two detectives as they held up their warrant cards.

'I'm busy. You'll have to come back later.'

Jan glanced over her shoulder, and then caught Turpin's eye.

He winked, then grew serious once more.

'Shop's empty,' he said. 'This won't take long.'

'Mind closing the counter?' Jan added. 'Easier to have a chat without this glass in the way, don't you think?'

Kath harrumphed, but reached across the counter and propped up a sign stating the post office was closed, then moved to a narrow door behind her and punched in a four-digit code. Moments later, she stood in front of Jan, arms folded across her ample chest.

'What do you want?'

'Is there somewhere we can talk in private?' Jan sensed the woman's hostility and resisted the urge to take a step back.

She had met Jack Russell dogs with less attitude.

Kath shrugged. 'I've got nothing to hide.'

'Where were you between the hours of seven o'clock on Saturday and eight o'clock the following morning when Seamus Carter's body was found?'

'What?'

'Answer the question please.'

'I was here, working late until about eight o'clock then I walked to the pub, where I met Martin.'

'Martin?'

'My husband.'

'When did you leave the pub?'

Kath pursed her lips, then exhaled. 'A little after eleven o'clock. After the band finished.'

'Did you leave the pub alone?'

'No – I told you. I was with my husband.'

'Where did you go when you left the pub?'

'Home, of course. Had to be up at five o'clock for the newspaper delivery, didn't I?'

'And your husband?'

'Snoring his head off when I left him.' Her eyes flitted between Jan and Turpin, a bewilderment emanating from her. 'Look, what's this about?'

'Did you leave the pub at any time between eight and eleven o'clock?'

'No – no, I didn't.'

'Do you have a set of keys to the church?' said Turpin.

'Why would I?'

He pointed to the notice next to the counter window. 'You offer key cutting services. Jim Aster confirmed he's supplied two sets in the past. Did you make another set without his knowledge?'

'No, of course not.'

'It would've been easy enough for you to do, wouldn't it? I mean, you only have part-time help here. No-one to see what you get up to when the shop's quiet, is there?'

'But I didn't.'

'Do you keep a record of the keys you cut here?' said Jan.

'We don't have to. I never took extra copies, honestly.' Kath's voice rose in pitch before she recovered and peered around them.

Jan followed her gaze to see a well-dressed woman approaching the end of the store.

As she drew closer, her brow furrowed. 'Oh, I'm sorry. I thought the post office was open.'

'Come back in ten minutes,' said Turpin.

The woman scuttled away, paused to speak to the teenager at the till, and then hurried outside.

Kath glared at them. 'I'm trying to run a business here.'

'And we're trying to solve two brutal murders and a serious assault,' said Jan, losing patience. 'How did you know Seamus Carter had his tongue removed?'

'Pardon? I don't—'

'Stop stalling, Kath. You told Gerald Aitchison that Seamus Carter's tongue was removed by his killer. Something that was previously only known to the emergency services who attended the scene and people investigating his murder. Of course, the only other person who would have been aware of this fact would be his killer. So, I'll ask you again. Did you leave the pub between the hours of eight and eleven o'clock?'

'No, I told you—'

'Did you go to the church between the hours of eleven o'clock that night and eight o'clock Sunday morning?'

'No! I didn't kill him!' She brought a hand to her mouth as if shocked at her outburst, her shoulders heaving.

'Then how did you know his tongue had been cut out?' said Jan.

Kath emitted a shuddering breath and dropped her hand. 'Helen told me. She overheard the police talking at the church after she found him.'

'Helen Wilson?'

'Yes.' Kath shrugged. 'She likes to gossip. Always has.'

'Seems like she's not the only one,' said Turpin, his eyes boring into Kath's.

She had the decency to blush, and looked away,

pulling a paper handkerchief from the sleeve of her cardigan.

'Next time, we'd appreciate it if you told us about matters involving our investigation,' said Jan. 'Not Gerald Aitchison. Not the press. Here's my card. Take it,' she added when Kath hesitated. 'And please inform us if you make any plans to leave the area before our enquiries are concluded. We'll want contact details for you at all times, is that clear?'

'Y-yes.' Kath took a step back. 'I'm sorry.'

'It's a bit bloody late for that,' said Jan, and followed Turpin to the door.

CHAPTER THIRTY-FIVE

Mark pushed the mug of tepid coffee across the low table and peered through the window of the atrium at a darkening sky.

The late-afternoon briefing had passed with little new information to support the theory he'd so confidently posited to DI Kennedy only the previous day, and a sense of panic was beginning to threaten common sense.

The brutality of the attacks, the audaciousness of the killer in his method of breaking into his victims' places of worship or homes, and the sheer lack of evidence or a suspect, was starting to manifest in an exhaustion that seeped into the investigative team.

It left Mark wrung out and on tenterhooks, wondering who would be next.

Because, surely, a killer with such bloodlust that

had been displayed to date would go on until he was stopped.

He turned back to the newspaper, avoiding the sensationalist reporting of the murders, and instead turned to the motoring section. His gaze skimmed blindly over the bright photographs and sales pitches that seemed out of place in a digital world, and more and more desperate in their copywriting techniques as he read on.

The fingers of his right hand clutched a scrunched up paper napkin, the meagre offering of a cold sausage roll from a vending machine doing little to counteract his hunger.

'Sarge?

He looked up from the sports headlines at Jan's voice, then sat upright as he took in the panicked expression on the detective constable's face as she hurried across the atrium to where he sat.

She dropped into the chair beside him and pushed aside the newspaper, ignoring his protests.

'Are you okay?' he said, gathering up the strewn pages.

She shoved a stapled collection of papers at him, then stabbed her forefinger on the bottom paragraph of the first page.

'What Dean Harper said to us when we

interviewed him. He said that no-one let on that they heard or saw anything.'

'Right. So, no-one would believe our killer if he tried to report whatever was going on all those years ago.'

'Yes, I know, but that's not my point. They didn't say, hear or see anything.'

Mark sat back in his chair, confused.

Jan exhaled, snatched back the papers and flicked through them until she reached the last page. 'Listen. It's the three wise monkeys, isn't it?'

'Is it?'

'Speak no evil, hear no evil, see no evil.'

A rush of air left his lungs as the realisation hit him and he saw the excitement in her eyes. 'Bloody hell.'

'I'm right, aren't I?'

'Has anyone had a chance to go through what we've got to date, to see if the three priests met at some point?'

'I've got Caroline working on it upstairs. I figured the same thing – if there's a convergence in their past, it might give us a lead in relation to a potential suspect.'

'Agreed. Something triggered this. Any word from the hospital on how Robert Argyle is doing?'

'I haven't heard anything.'

Mark checked his watch. 'Is Kennedy in?'

'He left twenty minutes ago. Said he's taking his wife out to dinner for their anniversary.'

He ran a hand over his jaw, stubble scratching his fingertips.

'The DI did say to phone him if anything urgent came up,' said Jan.

'Fair enough, but we need to corroborate this first.'

'Well, if it helps, and with respect, Sarge – I don't think these murders are about ensuring their silence, or that our priests were the abusers either.'

'Go on.'

'Well, if there was a conspiracy around what was happening then surely our killer would've done something about it years ago, rather than now?'

'So, what are you thinking?'

'Maybe he thinks they should be killed because they *didn't* say anything.'

'But why?'

Jan shook her head. 'I'm not sure yet. But that's not what's worrying me. There's a fourth monkey.'

'Since when?'

'It's not always cited, but I did some digging around to test my theory. Sometimes, there's a fourth monkey whose raison d'être is "do no evil".'

A sense of dread began to crawl within Mark's gut. 'You're saying our killer isn't finished?'

'No. I don't think so.'

He took the pages from her shaking hand, casting his eyes over the content as he tried to catch up.

She beat him to it. 'Mark – if I'm right, in some variations of the fourth monkey, he's shown as crossing his arms or covering his genitals. If our theory is correct and this is all about our priests trying to cover up systematic abuse, then we need to find out who our fourth victim is before it's too late. Before he loses his—'

Mark held up his hands and blinked, trying to lose the picture that was forming in his head.

'Get onto the hospital,' he said. 'We need to interview Robert Argyle as soon as possible.'

She pushed back her chair and snatched the paperwork from him.

'Jan?' He reached out for her hand to stop her, and grinned.

'What?'

'Good work.'

CHAPTER THIRTY-SIX

Robert Argyle groaned as the pain swept over him, tearing him from his slumber in an instant.

He blinked while he tried to get his bearings, and wondered why he was lying on his back in a brightly lit room.

A percussive *beep* to the left of him set his heart rate skywards as he remembered he was in a hospital bed. Memories from the attack resurfaced, and he whimpered.

He was thankful that the staff had managed to find him a private room – a rarity in the busy city hospital. He couldn't bear the inquisitive and furtive glances from fellow patients, for surely they would hear of his attack and the rumours would begin.

He reached up to his throat, and a bolt of fear clutched at his heart.

Where was his collar?

He sat upright and cast his gaze to the bedside table, a water jug and plastic beaker on a tray taking up most of the room, and then he reached out and opened the drawer underneath.

He exhaled. Both his collar and his wristwatch lay in the drawer.

'Morning, Father.'

He turned at the sound of the chirpy voice to see one of the nurses poking her head around the door frame.

'Hello.'

'I've got a couple of police detectives here that want to speak to you. That okay?'

He cleared his throat. 'Of course. Please, send them in.'

The nurse moved to one side, and a man in a grey department store suit stepped forward, his hand outstretched as he made the introductions.

'All things considered, Mr Argyle, you're looking well.'

He managed a smile as he shook hands with DS Turpin and then his female colleague before waving them to the visitor chairs at the side of the bed.

'It's "Father", not "Mister",' he said, but not unkindly. 'And thank you.'

'We've taken a look at the statement you've already

provided, and wondered if you could answer some questions?' said Jan.

'Of course.' He shuffled backwards, adjusted the pillows behind his shoulders, then folded his hands in his lap.

'Could you take us through the events of the night you were attacked?'

'You said you've read my statement.'

'It's in case anything new comes to light,' she said. 'Something that might've been overlooked previously, with everything else that was going on.'

'Ah, I see.'

On cue, the area where his earlobe had once been flared painfully and as he emitted a grunt of pain, Turpin leaned forward, his eyes full of concern.

'Do you need the nurse?'

He held up a hand, and shook his head. 'No, that's okay. I had some painkillers a little while ago. Sorry – where were we?'

'The events of that night.'

He shivered. 'I had no idea there was someone else in the house, until I heard a noise upstairs. Stupid, really. I mean, I suppose I was tired. Too much fresh air from working in the garden all afternoon, and by the time I'd sat down all I wanted to do was enjoy a drink before I started on the paperwork. That's when I heard it – it sounded like something had tumbled onto the carpet in the room above. I knew I hadn't left any windows open. I spent most of my housekeeping budget last week on new locks.'

'How do you think your attacker got in?' said Jan.

'Through the back door while I was messing about in the garden. Brazen really, wasn't it? Must've walked straight in and gone upstairs to wait.'

'You didn't notice anything when you went back inside?'

'No. Like I said, I was tired. And you don't expect to be attacked in your own home, do you?'

Neither of the detectives said a word, and he shrugged. 'I didn't anyway. Not here.'

'You said you heard a noise first?'

'I think right then I knew I was in trouble, but I don't know – I froze. I couldn't move. Moments later, the door that leads out to the hallway burst open, and he—' He broke off, ashamed at the shuddering breath that escaped his lips. 'He moved so fast. I didn't have time to stand up, and then he got the rope around my neck and started pulling me backwards against the armchair. I was twisting my head, trying to loosen it, and then he held a knife in front of my face.' A tear escaped and rolled down his cheek. 'I was terrified. I'd heard what happened to the other two, and I didn't want to die like that. The pain— the pain was unbearable when he began to cut me.'

'How did you escape?'

'Something in me snapped, and I lashed out. I managed to hit him on the soft skin below the elbow joint, and he dropped the knife.'

'Lucky.'

He managed a faint smile. 'Not really. I used to run a mission in a suburb of Lagos when I was younger. I took some self-defence lessons in my spare time and helped to teach some of the younger children basic karate. Gave them a better chance of surviving on the streets, or at least I hoped it did. Guess I haven't forgotten some of the old kata after all.'

'Back to the other night,' said Turpin. 'What happened next?'

'I've no idea why I remembered it when I did, but I was angry, too. He seemed taken aback by what I'd done – his hand was shaking when he bent down to pick up the knife, and by then I was on my feet. That's when he ran – straight out the front door.'

Jan stopped writing, her pen poised above her notebook. 'None of your neighbours reported seeing anyone leave.'

'He was wearing dark-coloured clothing, and, believe me, he didn't hang around. I ran out after him but by the time I got to the end of the path, he'd already disappeared around the corner. That's when I went back inside and called the police.'

'Did you hear a car engine, or anything like that?'

'No – I don't remember. I don't think so.'

'Did your attacker say anything?'

'No.'

'What about any distinguishing features?'

He shook his head. 'He was wearing a mask – one of those black woollen things with holes for his eyes.'

'A balaclava?'

'That's it. And gloves. Like the ones you see on the telly when there's a crime.' He felt his cheeks redden. 'I mean, I suppose you wear those, too.'

Turpin shuffled in his seat, and Robert realised the hard plastic was probably uncomfortable. The detective gave up, and instead rose to his feet and wandered across to the window that looked out over one of the hospital's two car parks. He turned and leaned against the sill.

'Did you know either Seamus Carter or Philip Baxter?'

'Not personally. I met them at a couple of functions over the years – meetings at the diocesan office, that sort of thing.'

'Had you received any threats prior to being attacked?'

'No, nothing at all.'

'Nothing in the post, no phone calls that gave you cause for concern?'

'No.'

Argyle watched as the detective looked away, his face troubled, and he realised that despite everything he'd read in the local newspapers and seen on the television, the police had no idea why two men had been murdered and himself attacked.

And as they said their goodbyes and wished him a speedy recovery, his thoughts returned to the secrets he kept, and his heart ached with loneliness.

For there was no-one he could talk to, no-one he could confide in and, even if there was, he wouldn't.

CHAPTER THIRTY-SEVEN

Mark chucked the car keys on the desk and watched dispassionately as they bounced across the varnished surface and then slid onto the carpet.

Jan emitted a sigh as she sank into her seat and their eyes met across their computer screens.

His thoughts echoed her frustration, but he remained quiet and instead busied himself working through the voicemail messages that had been left on his desk phone by people who hadn't yet obtained his mobile number.

He wondered how long the temporary respite would last. Replacing the receiver after scribbling down the last notes and deleting the final message, he glanced up at the sound of his name to see Jan waving her phone at him.

'What's up?'

'Tom, down on the front desk. Says he's got someone down there – a bloke – who wants to speak to us about Seamus Carter. Apparently, he's very agitated and won't speak to uniform. He's been here since nine o'clock.'

Mark checked his watch. 'Three hours? All right – tell Tom we'll be right down.'

Jan murmured into her phone as he shrugged on his jacket and straightened his tie, then gave him a nod as she gathered up her notebook and pen.

'According to Tom, this bloke sounds genuine so I don't think he's going for the celebrity angle.'

'Thank goodness.'

Mark had been waiting for exactly that. In his experience, there were often people who would seek to speak to the police simply so that they could tell friends and family – usually via social media – that they were a "witness" to a high-profile murder enquiry, and it rankled him.

He resisted the urge to cross his fingers and followed Jan out of the door.

When they entered the reception area of the police station, Tom was waiting for them and pointed his pen at a lone figure sitting in a plastic chair next to the glass doors.

'Goes by the name of Simon Parkes. I've got

interview room number six set aside for you for the next hour if you want it.'

'Thanks.'

Mark shoved his hands in his pockets and watched Parkes for a moment.

The man sat with his elbows on his knees, his head turned away from the desk. He hadn't even glanced around at the sound of voices and seemed lost in thought watching the passing traffic beyond the glass.

He'd placed a waxed jacket on the seat beside him, the green-coloured material faded and scuffed. His shoes were of a similar state, robust but well worn.

Mark tapped Jan on the arm and jerked his head.

Parkes finally turned to face them, straightening as he did so, and Mark was taken aback by his red-rimmed eyes. Despite this, he noticed the resemblance to the man described by Father Templeton and the subsequent sketch artist's impression.

The man rose to his feet as they drew near. 'Are you detectives?'

'We are.' Mark introduced Jan and then himself. 'I understand from our colleague here that you've been waiting for some time to speak with us. Can I ask why you didn't feel it appropriate to speak to one of our uniformed colleagues?'

Parkes leaned over and swept up his coat and

folded it over his left arm before answering. When he did, his voice shook.

'I needed to speak with someone who would listen.'

'Our officers are highly trained interviewers—'

A sad smile contorted Parkes's lip. 'I needed to speak to someone directly involved with the investigation.'

'Sergeant Wilcox said you knew Seamus Carter. Is that true?'

'It is.'

'All right, Mr Parkes. What would you like to speak to us about?'

'Seamus, of course. It's all my fault, you see.'

Mark caught Jan's shocked expression and then reached out and guided Parkes towards the corridor that led to the interview rooms, his mouth set.

'Stop talking right now. Come through here.'

He led the way past interview rooms one and two, his geographical knowledge of the layout not quite attuned yet to the way the doors had been numbered. Finally, he found the one Tom had booked for them.

Mark held open the door and waited while Parkes edged his way past and then took a seat facing the exit, the one that Mark preferred.

He wondered whether the manoeuvre was borne of habit or deliberate, then shook off the thought and berated himself for his paranoia.

Parkes had come to them, hadn't he? And from the way he plucked at a loose piece of skin on his left thumb, he wasn't looking forward to the discussion. Not the stance of a man who was seeking to protect himself.

Mark eased into the seat opposite Parkes while Jan flipped to a clean page of her notebook, pressed the "start" button on the recording equipment to the right of her and read out the formal caution for a witness interview.

That done, Mark leaned forward and tried to keep his features as open as possible, encouraging the other man's trust.

'What is it you wanted to discuss with us about Seamus?' he said. 'And why is it "all your fault"?'

Parkes released a shuddering breath and ran a hand over his face. 'I didn't kill anyone, all right? I just wanted to talk to you.'

'I'm all ears.'

Mark clasped his hands and waited, wondering if he'd made a mistake and that Parkes would simply be another local resident wanting information.

Parkes cleared his throat, and shuffled in his chair. His eyes dropped to the chipped surface of the table. 'I was hoping to speak to Seamus. That's why I came here. I thought he might be able to help after all this time.'

'Help in what way?'

'Speak out.' Parkes sighed and leaned back. 'And instead, I led his killer right to his door.'

Mark frowned. 'You'll need to give us a better explanation than that, Mr Parkes. How did you know Seamus Carter?'

'I was about thirteen when I first met him. He'd just joined the diocese – I'm not sure where he'd been before that. You'd have to ask his bosses, I guess. But he seemed friendly enough, if daunted by the job.'

'Hang on. Whereabouts are we talking about?'

'Bristol.'

Mark ignored the flutter in his chest. 'When was this?'

'Three years before it all happened.'

'What happened?'

Parkes shuffled in his seat, then crossed his arms over his chest and peered intently at the notebook in Jan's hand. 'He knew we were being abused, and he didn't say anything.'

Mark gave him a few seconds, then leaned forward. 'Could you start at the beginning, Mr Parkes? In your own time.'

The man's eyes flickered to his. 'There was a boy. Jeremy Wallace. There was a rumour going around a few years after I joined the choir. It was tradition in my family, see? All the boys got sent to choir. I was the eldest so my two brothers didn't join until afterwards. I don't know – I remember turning up the first day and thinking the choirmaster, Father Hennessy was – how to put it? – intense. That's it. Intense. He used to watch us like a hawk. Beady eyes. And he was a big bloke. Tall, but muscular I think, too. He took the physical exercise classes for the youth club.' Parkes shuddered, an uncontrollable spasm that wracked his body. 'I'd hate to think what he did to *them*.'

'What happened to the priest, Father Hennessy?' said Mark.

'His luck ran out eventually. He got caught and put away a few months after Jeremy's death.'

'We were made aware earlier this week that Jeremy Wallace killed himself, probably because of abuse he was suffering.'

'That's right.'

'And we understand that nothing was done to help Jeremy.'

'They all stayed silent. Me and some of the other boys tried to speak out about it. A few of us even used our confession to try to raise the alarm, but each of the priests we spoke to kept quiet. They never reported it. Then about nine months after Jeremy died, Hennessy made the mistake of choosing a boy whose uncle was in the police. Of course, then it all became an exercise in saving face within the parish.'

'What do you mean?'

'The diocese used the police investigation as an excuse to wipe everything else under the carpet. They never told the police about the other boys who had been abused. As far as the investigating officers were concerned, Hennessy had only abused the policeman's nephew and Jeremy Wallace.'

Jan leaned forward. 'Mr Parkes, when we spoke to the diocese, they volunteered no information about Father Hennessy being with them.'

He sneered at her. 'Of course they didn't – he was ex-communicated before his case came to court. They washed their hands of him and moved on.'

'How come you waited until now to ask Seamus to speak out about the abuse if he knew about it all those years ago?' said Mark.

'Because Hennessy's sentence got appealed last month. Unless someone from the Church speaks out about the abuse he wasn't convicted for back then, he's going to be free within weeks. They reduced his sentence for good behaviour. *Good behaviour*.' The man's voice trembled. 'Seamus was the only person I could think of who could help. He knew about the original abuse, but he didn't say anything at the time. Now Hennessy will be released from prison – and he'll start abusing again, mark my words. A monster like that won't stop. Not after being locked away for so long.'

'Did you speak with Seamus Carter?'

'Eventually, yes. I went to the church a few weeks ago. He didn't look pleased to see me, but he couldn't refuse my request for him to hear my confession. That's when I asked him again to help. He mumbled something, then told me what my penance was. That was it. I left after that. When I didn't hear from him again after a few days, I left a message on his answer phone, but he never returned it. He just ignored me. Again.'

'Mr Parkes, did you know a priest called Philip Baxter?'

The man nodded. 'I did, yes. I tried to contact him as well. He's dead, isn't he? I saw it on the news.'

'How did you know him?'

Parkes hunched forwards, his voice falling to a whisper. 'He knew. He was there. When it all happened. I was older than the boy who was being abused, but I could see how Hennessy was looking at me. I knew I'd be next. I'd moved from Cardiff with my parents into the area about six months before. As soon as he grew bored with Jeremy, he'd start on me because I was new. And I knew my parents wouldn't believe me either. I tried telling Baxter after practice one evening – I nearly ran into him trying to get out of there before Hennessy had a chance to get me alone. I told him what was happening, and he said he'd look into it, but he did nothing. Nothing at all. Jeremy died, and no-one gave a shit about him. None of them gave a shit about any of us.'

Mark glanced over at Jan, then turned back to Parkes.

'We're going to need a list of everyone else you spoke to about Seamus Carter, but first – where were you on the nights of his and Philip Baxter's deaths?'

CHAPTER THIRTY-EIGHT

DI Kennedy paced in front of the whiteboard as Mark and Jan updated the rest of the team about their interview with Simon Parkes, then began the hastily arranged briefing as they took their seats.

'So, thanks to Mr Parkes, we finally have a motive for our killer,' he said, and turned to face the photographs and timeline that had been constructed over the past few days. 'You were right, Jan – it seems these men are being targeted for staying silent about the systematic abuse that was taking place in the parish north of Bristol.'

He shook his head and faced the team once more. 'It's a breakthrough, but we still have a long way to go. I want that list of names from Parkes shared out between you. Track down every single one of them, arrange interviews via local uniform from Avon and Somerset where you're not satisfied with a phone call and find out their movements on the night of Carter's and Baxter's deaths, as well as the attack on Robert Argyle.'

Jan scribbled a note to herself and leaned across to Caroline as the young detective flapped a page from the HOLMES2 database at her.

'What is it, you two?' said Kennedy.

'Guv – we still need to ascertain if the killer has a fourth victim in mind, based on Jan's theory,' said Caroline.

'When we spoke with Parkes, we asked him whether he knows who the fourth target might be,' said Jan. 'He has no idea.'

'No names on the list he gave us correlated with any known persons in the database to date,' added Turpin. 'So, at the present time, our potential fourth victim is an unknown.'

'And we have no way of warning them that their life may be in danger.' Kennedy swore under his breath and tugged at his tie, throwing it onto a desk nearby. 'All right, what about the diocesan office? Jan, have you got the list of curates and priests from Seamus's time there?'

'They haven't sent it yet, guv.'

'Do you think they're stalling to protect themselves?'

She shrugged. 'Maybe. But it could be the case that

a lot of their records are kept manually and not in one central location that's causing the delay.'

'Get back onto them after this briefing and chase it up. Tell them we believe someone's life is in danger and it's imperative we have that information today – even if it's an incomplete list. At least it'll give us something to get started with. Once you've got it, check it against anyone who might have moved from Bristol to this area. At least we might be able to narrow down our focus that way.'

'Guv.'

'What do we know about George Hennessy, this ex-communicated priest who's up for a parole hearing?'

'Imprisoned after a boy he abused reported it to his father. For once it got taken seriously – unlike the accusations we've heard Jeremy Wallace made at the time,' said Mark. 'The kid had evidence, too, which probably helped convince the parents. He took a handheld Dictaphone his dad kept in the study at home and recorded what was done to him – including the threats that were directed at his younger brother if he didn't keep quiet.'

'So, it forced the diocese's hand,' said Kennedy.

'The police turned up at Hennessy's house that night,' said Mark. 'The first the bishop heard about that last complaint was when he received a phone call from the priest requesting legal representation.'

'What about the other priests in the diocese?' said Caroline. 'The ones like Seamus Carter who stayed silent even though they knew?'

Jan shook her head. 'We've been through the transcripts from the interviews at the time. There wasn't enough evidence to charge them, especially as the Church closed ranks once it was determined some of the boys had only ever mentioned the abuse when they were in confession. Avon and Somerset Police were met with a wall of silence – they had nothing to work with.'

'Which is why our killer might be taking the matter into his own hands,' Mark added.

'All right,' said Kennedy. 'McClellan – get onto the prison and find out what visitors this ex-communicated priest has had over the years. Find out whether he's got family – anything that'll give us a lead.'

A loud sniff emanated from the back of the room. 'Will do, guv.'

'Do you think the killer might've visited him?' said Jan.

'Maybe, even though it's a long shot,' said Kennedy. 'At least once we've got those names we'll be able to cross-reference them against the ones Parkes has given to us.' He checked his watch. 'Okay, we'll end there. You've got plenty to do. I realise you've all been working some long hours on this investigation but we've got enough evidence to suggest that our killer isn't finished yet. Get to work.'

Jan hurried over to her computer and tried not to look at the time displayed in the lower corner of the screen.

Instead, she turned her attention to the names she'd been allocated, picked up her phone and took a deep breath.

Surely someone out there could give them the breakthrough they so desperately needed?

CHAPTER THIRTY-NINE

Mark took a step back and swore as the temperamental coffee machine spat the last dregs of dark-brown liquid over his shoes.

He sighed, placed his mug on the counter and plucked a handful of paper towels off a roll that had been left upright next to the offending machine by its last victim, then wiped away the mess.

As he threw the waste into the bin, his eyes fell on the clock above the door to the kitchenette and he frowned, realising with a shock that it was almost seven-thirty. He'd been so engrossed in reading through the database entries for the investigation to date that he'd lost track of time.

His stomach rumbled in protest.

Jan had left nearly two hours ago, citing a parent/teacher night she couldn't afford to miss. As he reached his desk, he leaned across and pinched a handful of biscuits from her supply, vowing to buy a replacement packet for her and ruing the diet he was trying to maintain.

He had a feeling it was all the food he was going to get tonight.

Slouching in his chair with a sigh, he glared at the computer screen and took a sip of coffee, grimacing as the bitter flavour soured his taste buds, then shoved half a biscuit in his mouth and leaned closer, his hand moving the mouse through the file links.

If he was honest, he didn't really know what he was looking for.

He knew he didn't want to go back to the boat yet. Hamish would scrounge supper from a neighbour if he was peckish, and Mark couldn't shake a niggling sensation that had been bothering him since they'd spoken with Robert Argyle.

With his chin in his hand, his eyes roamed over the images from the first crime scene that had been uploaded to the HOLMES2 database by one of the administrative staff earlier in the investigation. His top lip curled as he took in the grisly scene, the photographs flickering past one after the other, highlighting different angles of Seamus Carter's butchered face and neck.

Reaching out for his coffee, he clicked his mouse to move on to the next sequence of images.

His hand froze above the steaming drink, his heart skipping a beat.

'What the f—'

His coffee forgotten, Mark shuffled forward on his chair and peered closer at the screen, his eyes seeking out the controls to enlarge the image.

That done, it took another second for his brain to react to what was in front of him.

He checked the date in the top right-hand corner of the file name, then flicked back to the previous image he'd seen.

The first photograph was one of Seamus Carter taken at the crime scene, a close-up of his jawline showing the damage caused by his killer.

The second one was a photograph taken by Clive Moore after Gillian Appleworth had concluded Philip Baxter's post mortem and he'd washed the body prior to final arrangements being made for the priest's funeral.

Clive had caught the same angle as the CSI photographer had with Seamus Carter's face, although Mark suspected this was more by luck than design.

What it showed sent a chill across his shoulders before he sprang into action.

He began to search through the entries in the

HOLMES2 database, cursing his inability to remember phone numbers while his eyes flickered over the titles of the different files that had been uploaded, desperately forcing himself to slow down so he didn't overlook the one he sought.

After what seemed an age and several attempts getting used to how his new colleagues in Thames Valley Police filed their supporting documentation into the database, he found what he was looking for and dialled the number while pacing the carpet.

'This is Gillian Appleworth—'

'Gillian – don't hang up. It's Mark Turpin—'

'—I can't get to the phone right now, but if you leave a message I'll get back to you as soon as possible.'

'Shit.'

Mark ended the call and flung the mobile phone across his desk, running a hand over his mouth as his eyes fell upon the images on his screen once more.

He knew he was right.

They had all missed it – himself included. But, there it was – staring at him, the photographer's lens catching the minute detail.

Pure chance was often all that stood between an investigative team and a breakthrough, and his gut told him he was onto something.

A thought struck him and he waggled his finger in the air as he threw himself into his chair.

Launching himself at the keyboard, he opened a search engine and typed in a keyword string.

Surely there had to be another Home Office pathologist nearby he could ask?

A results page sprang to life on the screen, and he clicked on the second link, mentally crossing his fingers while he let loose a string of expletives.

Only seven pathologists covered an area that encompassed Greater London, the South East and West Midlands – and none of them were within a two-hour drive of where he sat.

He pushed back his chair, debating his options and then exhaled and grabbed his car keys.

'This could go one of two ways,' he muttered, and headed out of the door at a run.

CHAPTER FORTY

Mark ratcheted the handbrake lever and stared out of the windscreen at the Georgian house in front of him.

A gust of wind rocked the car and he removed the keys from the ignition, shoving open the door.

Despite the reputation of the village where Gillian and her husband lived, he wasn't taking any chances with the pool car, and so he thumbed the key fob to lock the doors and hugged his arms to his chest as he ran towards the front door.

Heavy curtains covered the windows at the front of the property, but chinks of light escaped through the panes of the glass to the left of the paved garden path.

As with most houses of the period, the converted farmhouse had a portico jutting out from the front door and Mark sheltered under it from the late spring storm while waiting for the doorbell to be answered.

Movement caught his attention, a footfall scuffing on the parquet flooring he knew lined the hallway beyond the oak door, and he cleared his throat in anticipation while straightening his tie.

He squinted as the light above his head blinked to life, and then the door was opened – not much, just enough for Gillian's husband, Alistair, to peer around, his forehead creased.

'Mark? What are you doing here?'

'Sorry, Alistair. I tried to phone ahead, but—'

'What do you want? Is everything okay?'

'Yes, yes – everything's fine. I wondered if I might have a word with Gillian?'

'We're about to sit down to dinner.'

'It's urgent.'

'This is a bit out of the blue.'

Mark forced a smile, his patience beginning to wane. 'It usually is with a murder investigation.'

Alistair's shoulders dropped. 'I see. You'd better come inside.'

Mark stepped over the threshold, his senses honing in on the aroma of a Thai curry while his stomach rumbled. Memories of Gillian's famous recipe stung his taste buds, and he swallowed to lose the sensation.

'Wait here. I'll go and get her.'

'Thanks, Alistair.' He fought down the disappointment that rose in his chest as the man disappeared along the hallway towards the kitchen. Before the attack in Swindon, before he split up with Debbie, he'd have been welcomed into the Appleworths' home with enthusiasm, but it seemed Gillian's antipathy towards him had rubbed off on her husband who was now reluctant to share his home with his ex-brother-in-law.

He turned away from the retreating figure and focused on the watercolours that adorned the entrance hallway and staircase.

Stepping closer, he recognised Gillian's light touch with a brush – she and Debbie had shared the same talent for painting, with Debbie preferring the bold strokes of oil over watercolour.

'What are you doing here?'

He spun around at Gillian's voice.

The pathologist dried her hands on a towel as she advanced towards him, her face contorted with ill-disguised anger.

Instinctively, he raised his hands. 'I only want five minutes of your time.'

'Couldn't it wait until the morning?'

He felt the last of his patience draining from him. 'It could, but given what I've discovered could have a derogatory impact on your future career and reputation, I thought it might be better to have this conversation in private.'

She stopped dead. 'What did you say?'

'You heard me. Now, can we talk as civilised people or do you want to wait until you hear from your boss after my DI phones him in the morning with a formal complaint?'

She slapped the towel over the stair bannister and glared at him, her jaw working. After a moment, she took a deep breath and gestured towards the back of the house. 'Come through to the study.'

'Thank you.'

'This had better be good,' she said, as she brushed past him.

Mark trailed after her, biting back his rising anger. He had to remain professional, had to stay calm in order to seek Gillian's consensus with his theory. Despite their differences, he still respected her intellect, and it was to this he knew he'd have to appeal.

Gillian reached out automatically for a switch to the left as she pushed open the door, a series of spotlights illuminating her workspace. She gestured to one of two chairs next to a well-used desk strewn with paperwork, then turned and leaned against the teak surface and appraised him.

'That curry is going to be ready in fifteen minutes, so start talking.'

In reply, Mark reached inside his jacket and

removed the documentation he'd brought from the incident room, then handed her the photographs.

She raised an eyebrow as she took them, her brow furrowing further while she cast her eyes over the images. 'These are the ones I sent to DI Kennedy with my report for the two murdered priests. I'm presuming the others were taken by one of Jasper's team?'

'They were.'

'What's your point?' she said, thrusting them back towards him.

He ignored the photographs and watched her face. 'Your reports missed something.'

'What?'

'Take another look. Tell me what you see.'

She huffed in response, but to her credit sifted through the images once more. As the last photograph passed through her fingers, she shook her head and raised her eyes to his.

'Nothing I haven't seen before.'

He rose from his seat, reached behind her, and plucked up a magnifying glass from her desk, one he knew she'd inherited from her father. 'Use this.'

'Is this some sort of game, Mark? Because I really don't have time. I—'

'Shut up and look again. With this.'

Danger flashed in her eyes as she snatched the magnifying glass from him.

One, two, three photographs passed through her hands as she peered at the details, her practised eyes running over the images of the two dead priests whose post mortems she'd conducted within days of each other.

He didn't blame her – wouldn't blame her – for her incredulousness, but he did want her acknowledgement that he was right, and that she would help him.

He held his breath and waited.

The skin beneath her right eye twitched, and he exhaled some of the tension that had held him in thrall.

'Oh my God.' Her head jerked up, as confusion filled her eyes.

'Do you see it?'

In response, she strode across to an old dining table she used as a working space, swept a series of reports to one side, and spread out the photographs across the surface. Resting her hands on the table, she peered over her shoulder at him.

'Come over here.'

Mark pushed himself out of the chair and joined her. 'What do you think?'

'I-I don't know what to say.' Her voice shook. 'How did I miss this?'

A wave of pity swept over him, and he sighed. 'You're overworked, understaffed, and under pressure.'

'Don't make excuses for me, Mark.' She ran a hand through her hair, tipped her head back and blinked. 'All right. What's going through your mind? Do you want my resignation?'

'What?'

Her eyes met his, a steely gaze that didn't falter. 'Is that why you're here? To give me the bad news personally?'

'What sort of person do you take me for, Gillian?' Mark turned away and gestured at the photographs, his voice softening. 'That's the last thing I'd do. No, I need your help. This mark on their cheeks, it's tiny isn't it? Any ideas what could've made it?'

Gillian picked up a close-up of Seamus Carter's face, tracing her thumb over the man's cheek. 'When I saw this on our first victim, I thought he'd simply scratched the skin with a jagged thumbnail, or caught it while shaving. It's subtle compared to the bruises and scratches we attributed to his murder, see?'

'Is that why it didn't give you much cause for concern?'

She swallowed, then nodded. 'Yes. It didn't fit in with his other injuries because it's not deep – this red mark isn't as indented in the skin, which led me to believe it wasn't anything to do with the attack.'

She replaced the photograph while Mark selected an image taken at a similar angle of Philip Baxter's face. As he held it up, she wrung her hands. 'Shit, Mark. This is bad. This is really bad. I could lose everything over this.'

Mark paused, the photograph in his hand. It was the first time he'd ever heard Gillian sound scared.

She stared at the other images scattered across the table, her expression blank, her face pale under the artificial lighting.

'Gill? I meant what I said. I'm not going to tell anyone. I just want to stop the person who's been doing this, okay?'

'Everything all right in there?'

Mark jumped at the sound of Alistair's voice, and they both turned as the door opened.

Alistair peered around the frame, and cleared his throat. 'What did you want to do about dinner, Gill? Do you need me to do anything?'

Mark held his breath in the pause that followed, then Gillian spoke.

'Take it off the heat, darling. Just give it a stir now and again to make sure it doesn't stick. I can reheat it when we're done here. I'll make fresh rice. The dogs can have the overcooked rice for their breakfast tomorrow.'

'Oh. Okay. Will do.'

Her eyes met Mark's as Alistair retreated, her composure returning. 'Right. Where were we?'

He said nothing, staring at her hands.

'Mark?'

Mark held up the photograph to his line of sight, then looked at the pathologist's hands once more.

'Do you remove your rings when you're working, Gill?'

'What?' She peered down, splaying her fingers. 'Of course. The stone in my engagement ring tends to catch on the gloves otherwise, and I can't risk them tearing. I – oh.'

Mark snatched up her hand and ran his thumb over the stone. 'Does it turn on your finger easily?'

'Yes.' She twisted the ring around and turned her palm upwards.

He raised her hand so that it rested against his cheek, and pressed the stone against the skin as hard as he could.

When he released Gillian, her eyebrows shot upwards in realisation.

'It's not a man who's killing them, is it?' she said. 'It's a woman. Even wearing gloves, the ring she was wearing pierced their skin. But, even if I had left my rings on, I would've noticed. I wouldn't make the same mistake twice.'

'This isn't a mistake.' He paused. 'This looks like a message.'

Mark moved to the table, casting his eyes across the

sequence of images they'd laid out as the pieces began to drop into place.

'Can you take another look at the bodies in the morning? See if we're right?'

'Of course. What are you going to do?'

'I'm going to have another word with Robert Argyle as soon as the ward opens for visitors in the morning. See if he recalls anything that might help us now that we know what we're looking for.'

CHAPTER FORTY-ONE

Jan fought down a sense of shock as she listened to Turpin describe his conversation with Gillian Appleworth to DI Kennedy in a hurriedly arranged meeting the next morning.

He had phoned Jan while she was thrusting lunchboxes at the twins and trying to ascertain whether Luke had actually completed his homework on time. She'd answered with an exasperated "What?" before his words had silenced her.

Now here she was, third coffee of the morning in her grip, the twins dispatched to school thanks to their dad, and her trying to take down notes as her DS churned out his update as rapidly as machine-gun fire.

Where previously she'd sensed a reluctance in him to voice his opinions too much within the confines of the incident room, as if he were cognisant of being the new face on the team, he now strode in front of Kennedy's desk, gesticulating enthusiastically as he described what he'd been working on while the rest of them had been sleeping.

At least he had the decency to look out of breath when he'd finished, although whether that was due to excitement or lack of oxygen was anyone's guess.

Finally, nearly a full five minutes after Turpin had completed his précis of events, the DI dropped his pen to the desk, removed his glasses and folded his hands over the photographs spread across the blotter in front of him.

'And Gillian concurs with your assessment of these images?'

'Absolutely, guv. She's currently over at the morgue conducting a further examination of both of our victims and assures me she'll phone through with her findings later this morning. Those findings should corroborate our theory.'

'Your theory, Mark.'

Jan caught the twinkle in Kennedy's eye.

'All right,' the DI continued. He gathered the photographs together and handed them back to Turpin. 'We'll run it side by side with the current investigation. I agree, it's an angle that has to be explored properly. We'll bring the rest of the team up to speed in this morning's briefing.'

'Thanks, guv.'

Turpin led the way out of the office back into the incident room, and Jan waited until they'd reached their desks.

'What did Gillian say when you spoke to her last night?' she said. 'She couldn't have been very impressed.'

He shrugged, and placed the photographs in a manila folder before shoving it into a tray next to his phone charger. 'Pretty shocked, once I'd had the chance to explain.'

'Must've felt good to knock her down a peg or two after what she's been like to you.'

As soon as the words passed her lips, she knew she'd read him wrong.

Disappointment clouded his features, and he gave a slight shrug, a sadness emanating from him.

'Not at all,' he said. He waited until she'd pulled out a chair. 'She was horrified. Despite what she says about me, we were close once. We used to have a laugh together.'

'What happened?'

'She took umbrage at the fact Debbie and I split up, that's all. But whereas Debbie has managed to move on, Gillian's never forgiven me. She's a good pathologist though. Knows her stuff.'

'So why didn't she spot this?'

He looked away. 'We all make mistakes.'

Something in his words made Jan realise he wasn't going to share anything further with her and she decided not to press the point.

As she hurriedly checked her emails, she ignored the steady stream of team members entering the incident room and instead glanced across the computer screens to where Turpin sat, his brow furrowed as he worked.

Colour rose in her cheeks as she recalled the way in which Appleworth had spoken to him on their first day working together at the Upper Benham crime scene. She squared her shoulders and tried to concentrate on her emails, not sure that she'd be so forgiving in the same circumstances.

They had a potential breakthrough in their investigation though, one which hadn't been considered previously. Any recriminations about Gillian's mistakes – perceived or otherwise – could come later.

'Gather around.'

Kennedy's voice boomed across to where she sat, and Jan grabbed her notebook and pen before joining her colleagues for the briefing.

After collating updates from the detectives leading each group of investigators, he gestured to Turpin and explained the reasons for the additional angle of enquiry that would now take place.

A collective murmur filled the room at the news, and Jan noticed a few sideways glances at her colleague.

No doubt a few others shared her view about the pathologist, but to their credit no-one made any wisecracks and the briefing was concluded shortly after.

Kennedy gestured for Turpin to wait while the other team members moved back to their desks, and waved Jan over.

'You've probably already thought of it, but can you two go and speak to Robert Argyle this morning? See if he can recall anything that might support this theory of yours.'

'I had the distinct impression he wasn't telling us everything,' said Turpin.

Jan nodded. 'He's right. I was going over his witness statements again this morning and something doesn't gel about what he said regarding knowing the other two victims.'

'Agreed,' said Kennedy. 'Let me know what you find out.'

CHAPTER FORTY-TWO

Mark held out his arm to stop Jan in her tracks as they finished climbing the stairs and entered the hospital wing.

'What?'

'Do you mind if I lead this one?'

'Why? What are you thinking?'

He ran a hand over his head, then guided her out of the way of a hospital orderly pushing a wheelchair-bound elderly woman.

The woman smiled at them as she and her aide passed, then Mark lowered his voice.

'He's a bloke, who's used to living on his own. I've been wondering if he's simply too embarrassed to want to say too much in front of a woman.'

Jan opened her mouth to protest, then closed it.

'Shit, maybe you're right. I hadn't thought of that. Okay – how do you want to do this?'

'We'll start together. If I think he's stalling or withholding information, I'll give you a signal. Wait outside when I do, and give me a couple of minutes.'

'Sounds good.'

'Thanks.' He smiled. 'Some detectives wouldn't like the idea of being left out of the loop.'

'Some detectives need to get their heads out of their arses, then. I want to catch the bastard who's doing this as much as you.'

'Love your work, West.'

She grinned. 'Lead the way.'

He spun on his heel and headed towards the nurses' station at the end of the corridor, flicked open his warrant card and introduced themselves to the ward sister.

'Back again?' she said good-naturedly. 'Just in time, too. Visiting hours are up in half an hour.'

'How's he doing?' said Jan.

'Healing nicely. And he's so polite – I wish all our patients were like that.'

'Okay to go in and see him?'

'Of course. You know where he is?'

'We do, thanks,' said Mark.

'Don't wear him out.'

Mark threw a wave over his shoulder and moved towards Argyle's room.

A uniformed officer climbed sleepily to his feet as they approached, easing out the cricks in his back muscles with a rueful smile.

'Bloody visitor chairs,' he said. 'They don't like you to get too comfortable around here, that's for sure.'

'Any problems?' said Jan.

'None whatsoever. Had a reporter sniffing around yesterday, but DC McClellan removed Argyle's name from the whiteboard at the nurse's station and on the door here yesterday, so he hasn't been disturbed. By the time we'd finished speaking with the reporter he was contemplating a new career anyway.'

He chuckled, the encounter evidently breaking up the monotony of the task at hand.

'No other visitors?' said Mark.

'No. Sad, isn't it? I mean the bloke spends all his life looking out for others, and none of them have bothered to drop by. There've been a few cards and some flowers, but that's it.' He shrugged. 'There haven't even been any visitors from his lot – you know, the church.'

Mark said nothing, but wondered whether Argyle's colleagues were ignoring him from embarrassment or a growing alarm at the murders and a fear of exposing a deeper problem within the organisation – that of an ex-communicated priest about to be released from prison, and a killer determined to level his or her own sense of justice against others in the Church for their years of silence about how much of his abuses went unreported.

Instead, he waved the uniformed officer back to his seat. 'We won't be in there long. Do you want us to fetch you a coffee or anything?'

'No – I'm fine, thanks. I've only got another hour or so before my shift change anyway.'

Mark crossed the floor and rapped his knuckles on the door, then pushed it open without waiting for a response.

Robert Argyle sat propped against two pillows, his thin sandy hair freshly washed but doing little to offset the vicious purple and yellow bruises that clustered around his nose and jawline.

Mark automatically cleared his throat at the sight of the jagged red line at the man's neck, but gave a slight shake of his head at the quizzical glance that Jan shot him.

He pushed the memories aside, forcing himself to concentrate on the interview ahead as he moved towards the bed and lowered himself into the visitor's chair beside it.

Jan hovered at the door, notebook and pen poised as the priest's gaze shifted between them, a wariness seeping into his eyes.

'Has something happened?' he said, a quaver in his voice.

'We have reason to believe that another man's life is in danger,' said Mark. 'And we're hoping you can shed some light on who that might be, given your past history.'

'Me?' Argyle's bloodshot eyes widened. 'In what way?'

'Bristol,' said Mark, and took some satisfaction from the shock that flitted across the priest's features. He edged closer, and leaned his elbows on his knees as he spoke. 'When we interviewed you yesterday, you told us that you didn't know either Seamus Carter or Philip Baxter very well. You gave us the impression you'd only bumped into them at a few formal functions at the diocesan office over the years. That's not the truth, is it?'

Argyle opened his mouth to speak, then clenched his jaw as his brow creased. He shook his head and lowered his eyes to his clasped hands.

'You were at Bristol with Seamus Carter, Philip Baxter, and a priest by the name of George Hennessy,' said Mark.

A shiver shook Argyle's shoulders, and he paled.

'I'd hoped never to hear that name again,' he whispered.

'He's due to be released from prison next month,' said Mark.

Argyle's head jerked up as his breath caught. 'That can't be possible. He was meant to be put away for years.'

'Apparently he's been very well behaved,' said Mark, unable to keep the sarcasm from his voice.

'But he's a monster!'

'And yet none of you mentioned that at the time. Do you recall a boy by the name of Jeremy Wallace?'

Argyle nodded.

'Do you remember what happened to him?'

'Yes.'

'And again, none of you reported it. In fact,' said Mark, fighting back disgust, 'none of you saw fit to take action against Hennessy until a young boy had the sense to record what was going on and report it to his parents.'

Argyle bit his lip. 'I couldn't say anything. The only time any of them spoke to me was during the sacrament of reconciliation. Jeremy spoke to Seamus and Philip, too, you know. They didn't do anything either. They—'

He broke off, and Mark spotted the spark of realisation seep into the other man's eyes.

'I do believe Father Argyle is catching up with us, DC West,' he said over his shoulder.

'About bloody time,' Jan muttered.

Mark turned back to the priest. 'We're working on the theory that your attacker, their killer, is delivering their own form of justice to punish you all for your silence. There were others who were abused that went unreported, weren't there? How many?'

'I don't know.'

'You must do,' said Mark. 'Those boys trusted you. They came to you for help. You were meant to protect them, but yet you said nothing. You remained silent.'

'The sacrament of reconciliation—'

'Bugger the sacrament,' Mark snarled, and shoved his chair back, jabbing his forefinger at the man. 'You protected a child molester.'

'I couldn't say anything!'

Argyle's voice rose to a wail, and Mark looked around as the door handle turned and the ward sister poked her head around the doorframe.

'What's going on in here?'

'Formal interview,' said Mark. 'Close the door, please.'

'He needs to rest.'

'He can catch up on his beauty sleep when I've finished. Close the door.' Mark whirled around to face Argyle. 'I want a list of names from you. Every person who knew about the abuse. The name of every kid who came to you for help who you ignored. All of them.'

'Why? What's going on?'

'Your attacker. Tell me again what happened.'

Argyle shook his head as if to try and catch up with the sudden change in direction Mark's questions were taking. 'L-like I said, before I had a chance to do anything, he had a noose around my neck and then waved a knife in front of my face.'

'Were you attacked from behind, or from the side?'

'From behind. I told you. I was sitting in my armchair. I heard a noise, and then the rope was over my head before I could react. He pulled, and I tried to loosen it from my neck. I realised that was futile, so I lashed out and punched him.'

'You're sure it was a man who attacked you?'

'Pardon?'

'Did your attacker speak to you, or make any noise to indicate that it was a man who was trying to kill you?'

'No – he didn't speak. He cried out when I punched him, though.'

'Cried out?'

Argyle's brow furrowed once more and he sank back into the pillows, his gaze tracing a framed print of a vase of flowers on the opposite wall. 'Oh.'

'What height was your attacker, would you say?'

'Average, I suppose. Not tall. Not short.'

'Guess.'

'I don't know. About five foot seven, maybe.'

'All right. What about build?'

'I've given all this information to the two police officers who were here the night I was brought in.'

'Humour me.'

'Slight. Thin. I was surprised actually when I lashed out. Thought he'd put up more of a fight, to be honest.'

'Unless he wasn't used to fighting. Unless it was a woman.'

Mark watched as Argyle processed the information, and then leaned closer and narrowed his eyes.

'There's a small bruise on your cheekbone. Do you recall anything pressing into your face while you were being attacked?'

'Um, no. No, I don't.'

'Think, Robert. It's important.'

Mark folded his arms over his chest as the priest closed his eyes, and tried not to let loose a torrent of expletives.

As far as he knew, there could be someone whose life was in danger right at this very moment, and yet Robert Argyle seemed oblivious to any sense of urgency – or remorse for his original silence.

'Something jabbed me when he – or she, maybe – grabbed my jaw, yes,' said Argyle eventually.

Mark glanced across to where Jan stood. 'Come over here.'

He was grateful to her that she didn't protest, and instead dropped her notebook and pen into her bag, joining him at the side of the bed.

'Give me your hand,' he said.

Mark grasped her by the wrist, and then gently turned the engagement ring on her left hand until it faced inwards, before holding it against Argyle's cheek and applying pressure.

'Like this?'

The priest's eyes opened wide.

'Yes. Like that.'

'Give me the names,' said Mark. 'Now.'

CHAPTER FORTY-THREE

Jan pulled her hair into a ponytail at the nape of her neck and raised her eyes to the growing display of photographs that were beginning to line the far wall of the incident room.

Since returning from the hospital, her shock and anguish at the number of boys' names Robert Argyle provided had transformed into a growing rage at what he and his colleagues had covered up.

Although he had provided names for some of the choirboys he remembered, he still refused to give any details of those who had sought his help through confession.

The amount of collusion within the diocese together with a defiance that their interpretation of faith should take precedence over the protection of those who were in their care shook her to her core.

She had clenched her fists as she'd listened to Argyle describe how he and the other priests had each been transposed to new parishes in order to guarantee their silence. He had seemed petulant that he'd only been able to see his old colleagues from time to time, and only under the watchful eye of the bishop and his cohorts at formal events.

Jan's frustration had been tempered when Turpin had informed Argyle to expect charges to be laid against him for remaining silent about the other abuses in the original case against Hennessy fifteen years ago, and that his current statement would be passed to the Parole Board considering the man's release.

'Here you go. Calmed down now?'

Jan turned and managed a faint smile as Turpin thrust a cup of tea at her.

'Getting there.' She pointed at the photographs. 'Any progress with these?'

'Caroline is still coordinating with uniform and working through the new information from the diocesan office,' he said. 'Nothing yet, but you know how it goes. We only need one person to give us a name that could push us in the right direction, but it's going to take time. We don't want to overlook something vital that could lead us to the killer – and her next victim.'

'We're running out of time, Mark. She'll kill again.'

'I know.'

He pulled a chair across to where she sat and slumped into it, frustration clouding his features. 'I can't help wondering if Philip Baxter would've lived if the diocese had told us about this when we first asked for information about Seamus instead of waiting until now to send it through.'

'Protecting themselves, I suppose,' said Jan. She sipped her tea.

'Yes, but not their own. They sacrificed Baxter rather than be embarrassed by what else Hennessy might've done all those years ago.' He clenched his fist. 'They'd rather set him free than make sure he stays locked away.'

Jan turned at movement to her left as DI Kennedy approached. 'Guv?'

'Let's get the team together,' he said. 'The Chief Superintendent has assigned half a dozen more uniformed officers to help us, so we'll have a quick briefing to go through what we've found so far and then see which tasks can be delegated to them.'

Jan pushed back her chair and wandered across to where a crowd of new faces joined the investigative team, Turpin traipsing after her.

She sensed an exhaustion in his movements, and cast her mind back to when they'd first met and how he'd been brought back to work sooner than his health might have allowed.

She pushed the thought aside, and concentrated on Kennedy as he began to introduce the new officers and conduct a review of the enquiry to date.

After a moment, he frowned and then called across the room. 'Caroline?'

Jan peered over her shoulder to see the detective constable staring at the wall of photographs, oblivious to the briefing and her colleagues.

'Caroline.'

The woman jumped at Kennedy's sharp tone, but pointed back to the whiteboard and held up a photograph in her other hand.

'I think I found him,' she said, her voice unsteady.

Turpin pushed away from the wall he'd been leaning against.

'The fourth victim?' he said, and took the photograph she held out to him.

'Yes,' said Caroline. Her gaze swept over her colleagues, her voice clear now that they were listening properly. 'I recognise the face from the list of names and profiles we got from the diocesan office after Jan chased them up again. He appears in Robert Argyle's list, too. Look, he's in this photograph from six years ago about a charity fundraiser at the diocesan office – that's him on the right, standing behind Philip Baxter.'

Jan hurried over to where Mark stood staring at the

second photograph that he had taken from Caroline, and peered at it.

'That's him, third row, second on the left, isn't it?' said Caroline.

'Where was this other photograph taken?' said Turpin.

'Bristol, seventeen years ago. It was taken by Dean Harper's father at a concert the choir gave – a big occasion, apparently. The whole choir stayed overnight after their performance and then travelled home the next day.'

'Have you got a name?' said Kennedy as he joined them.

'Terence Slade,' said Caroline. She gestured to the map she'd spread out over the table. 'Local priest for Balesford. It's the right area, isn't it? And we've got evidence that he was at Bristol at the same time as the others.'

Her eyes moved from Kennedy to Jan, her expression hopeful.

'We have to warn him before it's too late,' said Jan.

'It adds up,' said Turpin. 'What you think, guv?'

Kennedy pointed towards the door. 'Go.'

CHAPTER FORTY-FOUR

Father Terence Slade let the rosary beads move between his fingers as he recited the words by rote, and tried hard to concentrate on the verses that passed his lips.

His eyes flickered open, his heart racing as a gust of wind attacked the stained glass above the altar.

A bitter chill had clung to the countryside, late May delivering scant warm days and plenty of rain. The locals were already hedging their bets whether summer would bother making an appearance next month.

An ominous creaking sound reached his ears, and he realised with a sinking heart that he had forgotten to speak to the gardener that morning about lopping some branches off the two old yew trees on the other side of the solid brick wall that separated him from the churchyard.

He made a mental note to write it in his diary when he was back in his office at the plain house that served as his home once he had completed his religious duties for the evening.

Eventually, he stood and faced the rows of pews, smiling at the day's memories.

A busy morning in his parish had concluded with a lively afternoon wedding.

The betrothed couple had pleaded with him to let their dog attend the service, and he had happily agreed – he knew the old saying about never working with children or animals, but he secretly thought that the animals were a safer bet. As it was, the springer spaniel had nearly stolen the show, and he reckoned the ceremony ranked amongst his top five weddings in a role that had spanned nearly thirty years.

He had been the parish priest at Balesford for over fifteen of those years now, and compared to those of many of his peers, the parish boasted a healthy-sized congregation.

Of course, it helped that the church was also one of the smaller buildings in the diocese.

He descended the three shallow steps that lead down from the altar, the soles of his shoes echoing on the bare tiled floor. Muted light filled the space, a soft glow emanating from modern spotlights that had been set into the walls of the nave at regular intervals.

The effect was one of calmness, and he had resisted the urge to switch on the harsh overhead lights in order to savour the atmosphere. It was why, privately, he always enjoyed the service of the Friday evening Mass over any other. It was as if the working week was preparing itself for the day of celebration to come on the Sabbath. The encroaching twilight lent an intimacy to the proceedings that was sometimes missing from daytime services, and the cleansing nature of the readings and blessings soothed him after the sacrament of reconciliation.

Not that anyone chose to confess that night.

Shadows reached into the far corners of the nave, and he paused at a scurrying sound that reached his ears.

'Hello?'

Silence.

Another gust of wind shoved at the stained-glass windows, and he fought down the urge to cry out, rationalising instead that he knew the building inside out, and in fact had locked all the doors before taking his time to pray.

His mouth twitched as he realised that the noise was probably caused by the resident mouse.

He'd become quite fond of the little creature, even

giving it a name rather than face calling the local rodent control man employed by the diocese in the pastoral area.

'Run along, Oscar. There's nothing for you to eat here.'

No, he thought. That would be tomorrow, after the fête and all the kids from the local primary school received their share of the snacks and sweets that would be set aside as prizes for the various stalls.

Now, however, he wanted to relax, to read over the words he'd already written before printing them out ready for the morning. As much as he would've liked to read from his tablet computer, he wasn't sure how his older parishioners would react to the sight of such a modern monstrosity.

He couldn't get the man's voice out of his mind, though.

He was so sure it was him.

Three weeks ago, he had been paying for a tank of petrol at the filling station on the Oxford Road, oblivious to the people around him as he handed over his credit card and chatted with the cashier. It wasn't until he'd turned around, nodded to the man behind him without noticing his features, and started to weave his way past the queue of strangers to the door, that he'd heard him.

'Number four, please.'

He'd frozen, his hand on the door, but when he'd tried to peer around the others in the queue, he couldn't see the cashier or the man he'd acknowledged, his view was blocked.

'Excuse me.'

He'd apologised, held open the door for an elderly man with a stick, and then hurried to his car. He'd waited as long as he could, but an exasperated motorist behind him had honked his horn, and he'd had to pull away before the man whose voice he'd heard had emerged from the shop.

He was sure it was Simon Parkes, although he hadn't seen him since he was a teenager. Why was he here? Was he the reason Seamus Carter and Philip Baxter were dead?

He dropped the sheets of paper to his desk, and peered up at the crucifix.

He couldn't concentrate.

He leaned forward to adjust the music settings on the laptop, settling back into his chair as a concerto began to play. He closed his eyes, savouring the dulcet tones of the cello as it rose and fell, his shoulders relaxing as the orchestra swept him away.

He didn't hear the man enter the room.

CHAPTER FORTY-FIVE

'Excuse me. Father Slade?'

Mark staggered backwards as the man launched himself from his chair, brandishing a carved wooden letter opener, his mouth curled into a snarl.

The priest's eyes blazed, and Mark raised his hands.

'Jesus. Sorry – I didn't mean to frighten you.'

'Who are you?'

Mark lowered his hands to reach for his warrant card, his heart thrashing. 'Detective Sergeant Mark Turpin.'

He glanced over his shoulder at footsteps and then Jan appeared, her eyes widening as she took in the scene.

'Everything all right in here?'

The priest threw the letter opener onto the desk

and then glared at them both. 'You nearly gave me a heart attack.'

'I didn't mean to frighten you,' said Mark. 'But we have reason to suspect your life may be in danger.'

'Is there anyone else here?' said Jan.

'No. No – Beatrice, the cleaner left a while ago.' His face crumpled, weariness etched across his features. 'I thought I'd locked that door. What's going on?'

Mark motioned him back to his chair, and handed over a copy of the photograph Dean Harper's father had provided.

'Can you confirm this is you in this picture?'

Slade snatched the photograph from him, then emitted a shaking sigh. 'This is about the murders, isn't it?'

'Please answer the question.'

'Yes, it's me.' Slade handed back the photograph. 'Although I'd hoped never to be reminded of those times.'

'A little difficult, I would think, given we also have photographs of you from six years ago socialising with Seamus Carter, Philip Baxter, and Robert—'

'I didn't have a choice,' Slade snapped. 'It was all about keeping up appearances. I didn't want anything to do with them after what happened, but the diocesan office had other ideas.' His expression clouded. 'I wish I'd never said anything.'

Mark felt his stomach lurch. 'What do you mean?'

A sneer curled at Slade's top lip. 'Why do you think I got demoted to this backwater only to be followed by Carter's lot? They were sent here as a way to remind them to keep quiet about everything, but they were spying on me, too, just in case. I don't think the authorities – those in service to the bishop – trusted me with what I knew.'

'What did you know?'

'That George Hennessy was abusing boys in the choir. It had probably been going on for years by the time I arrived there. I found out about it by accident – spotted him afterwards one night, disgusting bastard.'

'Did you confront him?'

Slade shook his head. 'Have you met him?'

'Can't say I've had the pleasure.'

'He's a big bloke. I think he worked in construction or something as a teen before joining the church. No, I went straight to the bishop's office. They tried to deny anything was happening, of course. I thought they weren't going to do anything, then that boy came forward with the recording, and that was that.'

'There's nothing on the investigation file that mentions your name,' said Jan.

Slade snorted. 'They sent me here the minute

Hennessy was arrested. Too scared I'd speak to the police, I suppose. Of course, then I found out a few months later that I was going to be joined by Carter and that lot.' He shook his head, his gaze falling to the tiled floor. 'I thought I'd escape them, and the memories they brought.'

'How come you spoke out about the abuse taking place and they didn't?' said Mark.

'They were more senior than me, so I can only assume they found out from the boys taking the sacrament of reconciliation. They would never break the silence, whereas I was a witness to what was going on.'

Mark let the priest's words sink in as he paced the floor, his thoughts blurring.

He fought down the frustration and anger that threatened at Slade's admission that the Church had colluded to protect itself from the fallout following Hennessy's abuses, scattering the witnesses away from the Bristol area before the police had been able to question them, even though Slade had at least tried to raise the alarm.

He stopped and turned in the middle of the floor, ignored the quizzical look Jan shot him, and glared at Slade, who sat with his hands in his lap, a look of defeat etched in his eyes.

'Why didn't you go to the police at the time?' he

said. 'Why didn't you tell them what you'd seen?'

'I – I didn't need to. That's what they told me. When I heard Hennessy had been arrested, I contacted the diocesan office and asked if I'd be required to give a statement. They told me that there would be no need and that they'd already passed what I told them on to the police investigating the allegations.' His eyes moved from Mark to Jan, then back. 'They did, didn't they?'

Mark scratched at his jaw a moment. 'No, they didn't, Father,' he said softly. 'They didn't report the other abuses at all.'

'What?'

'We think that's why these killings are taking place. We think someone found out that Hennessy is going to be released early from prison because the church stayed silent about the other boys, and has decided to punish those who stayed silent all this time.'

Mark glanced across as the door to the sanctuary opened and a uniformed constable peered round.

'We've checked outside, Sarge. No sign of anyone.'

'Thank you.' Mark turned to Slade. 'PC Willis and his colleague will take you home and they'll stay with you until we deem it safe, is that understood?'

'I – I understand. Thank you.'

Jan stepped forward and pulled the photograph from her bag. 'Before you go – could you take a look at this, to see if you're able to recognise anyone else we should be speaking with?'

'Do you think your killer is still looking for someone?' said Slade.

'We do, yes,' said Mark. 'Given the victims to date were those who didn't speak out and report the abuse, but you did, we're fairly confident now that your life isn't in danger. You still get these two on guard duty in the meantime, though. I'm not taking any chances.'

Slade took the photograph from Jan and held it up to the light from his desk lamp.

After what seemed an age, he gave a grunt and tapped a finger on the image. 'Well, well. Who knew how well he'd turn out?'

He gave a smile.

Mark moved across to where he sat. 'What do you mean?'

'Don't you recognise him? This tall lad at the end of the back row.' Slade sighed as Mark snatched the photograph back and stared at it. 'Always wondered if he knew what was going on, given he was head choirboy.'

'Who is it?' said Jan.

'Gerald Aitchison. I thought he liked being head choirboy because he liked the prestige that came with the position. I suppose he never lost that sense of ambition, eh?'

CHAPTER FORTY-SIX

Mark ignored the squeak that caught in Jan's throat as he slewed the pool car through a left-hand bend and stomped on the accelerator when the road straightened out.

He had reached the car first, and she'd tossed the keys to him before programming Aitchison's address into the map app on her phone.

'Hell of a time for you to decide you want to drive,' she'd grumbled.

Now, the name of the village flashed by as he raced along the narrow lane, overgrown hedgerows slapping against the vehicle's paintwork.

He flinched as a branch snapped upon impact with the windscreen but the glass held.

Mark risked a glance across at Jan.

Jaw set, her expression determined, she peered

through the windscreen into the pitch-black beyond the reach of the headlights.

A gasp escaped her lips, and he turned his attention back to the road in time to see a fox dart across the road, narrowly missing the front wheels.

He resisted the urge to brake, and flexed his fingers on the steering wheel. 'Try his mobile number again.'

Jan's phone screen illuminated the passenger side of the car for a moment, and then a faint ringing reached him before the now familiar sound of Gerald Aitchison's voicemail message began.

'Nothing,' said Jan, dropping her hand to her lap, her grip firm on the phone. 'And uniform are over twenty minutes away.'

'Reach over and get the batons out. We're not waiting for them to get here.' Mark swore under his breath as they approached a crossroads and slowed the car. 'Which way?'

Jan squinted at the map on her phone. 'Left. It's only about a quarter of a mile away. His house should be this side of the village – keep a lookout for some metal gates and brick pillars.'

Mark accelerated. 'Landed gentry, is he?'

'Bought the place twelve years ago from what I read on his website. Farms potatoes and does quite well out of it, I think. Probably why he's popular with a lot of the other landowners in his constituency.'

They fell silent as Mark wrestled the vehicle round a final bend.

'Shit.'

Mark echoed Jan's expletive as he braked.

The gates to Aitchison's property were wide open, and as Mark steered the car up the short gravelled driveway, he noticed the front door lay open, light from a hallway spilling out over the threshold and onto a stone staircase.

'Stay behind me,' he ordered, then snatched one of the batons from Jan, launching himself from the car.

A white noise filled his ears as blood rushed to his head, and he staggered a moment.

'Mark?'

'I'm fine. Let's go.'

He flicked the baton away from him, the telescopic extension providing little in the way of protection but perhaps enough of a deterrent if needed.

The two-step *click* of a second baton over his shoulder was a welcome noise.

He had never doubted his colleague's determination during the short time they'd been working together, but deliberately walking into a dangerous situation without backup from their uniformed colleagues wasn't something he'd been planning.

'I'm ready,' Jan murmured.

He nodded in response, then hurried up the steps and into the house.

A silence greeted him, a sinister presence that caused the fine hairs at the back of his neck to tingle.

He held up a hand to Jan, and then a crash from the kitchen sent them running through the hallway to the back of the building.

Mark heard a door slam shut, and then the one in front of him was wrenched open.

He slid to a standstill on the tiled floor, his jaw slackening with shock.

'Penny?'

The florist's eyes widened, her mouth gaping as she held up her hands covered in blood.

Mark snapped to attention as Jan brushed past him, her voice commanding.

'Penny, where's Gerald?' she said. 'What have you done?'

'I – I tried to warn him. He wouldn't listen.' Penny Starling dropped her hand to her sides.

Mark stepped forward. 'What happened, Penny? Where is he?'

He could hear the urgency in his voice but fought down the rising panic.

The woman wore a blue shirt plastered with blood – evidently not her own, there was too much of it – and yet she seemed shocked.

Not the countenance of the brutal and sadistic killer he had been so desperately trying to stop.

'H– he's in the kitchen,' said Penny. 'I went to the loo, and then I heard a woman's voice. Please, help him—'

Mark took off after Jan, who had pushed past the woman and entered the room, her baton raised.

As he rounded the open door, his foot slid out from under him. His eyes fell to the slick of blood that covered the stone tiles and traced its origin to the man sitting slumped against the central worktop, his face pale as he clutched at his abdomen.

'Mr Aitchison?'

Jan dropped to a crouch, simultaneously pulling out her mobile phone.

Mark joined her and reached out for Aitchison's hand. 'Gerald, talk to me. Did Penny do this?'

The man's eyes flickered open, his gaze unfocused as a tear rolled down his cheek.

'Penny? No – Penny saved me.' He gasped, his body shaking. 'She walked in when – when...'

'Who attacked you?' said Mark, hearing the urgency in his voice.

Desperation crept into his thoughts. Aitchison had lost a lot of blood, and his hands were cold to Mark's touch.

He checked the floor beside them, but there was no knife, no weapon.

He turned back to Aitchison and gently prised the man's fingers away from his stomach, then bit back bile. He'd been stabbed, that much was certain, but his attacker had taken the weapon.

Mark straightened and pulled open drawers until he found a pile of neatly folded tea towels. He snatched up a handful and returned to Aitchison, ignoring the man's cries as he packed the material against the wound and placed the man's hands on top.

'Where's the ambulance?' he said to Jan as she lowered her phone.

'Fifteen minutes away.'

'Hang in there, Gerald. They're coming.'

Aitchison nodded, his eyes closing.

'Don't pass out yet,' said Mark, squeezing the man's shoulder. 'Where did she go? The person who did this to you?'

Aitchison blinked, a deep sigh escaping his lips. 'Out the back door. The yard backs onto a paddock.'

He spun on his heel and raced to the door.

'Mark!'

He turned, to see Jan advancing towards him, and shook his head.

'Stay here with him. Get Penny to sit in one of those chairs and get a statement from her.'

She swallowed and held out her baton. 'Be careful.'

He took the stick from her and headed into the night, blinking as his vision adjusted to the moonlit farmyard. Despite the urgency of the situation, he remained still, seeking out movement.

Whoever did this to Aitchison, whoever killed Seamus Carter and Philip Baxter before attacking Robert Argyle, would be panicking, he'd bet.

Sirens wailed in the distance, coming closer, and he hoped his colleague's request for additional uniformed backup had been actioned. He wanted to have the lane beyond the property closed as soon as possible to seal off a potential escape route.

The unexpected appearance of Penny Starling would have shocked his attacker, who had no doubt planned upon Aitchison being alone.

He was willing to bet there was no backup plan for his quarry. She would have killed Aitchison after mutilating him and calmly left the house afterwards without a trace. At some point, they would have to find her vehicle, but given the driveway was empty and no car engine had sounded when he was inside the house, he felt confident that she was on foot.

Movement at the edge of a barn on the boundary with the darkened paddock caught his eye, and he held his breath.

The approaching sirens had forced the killer's

hand, and now Mark waited to see which it would be – fight or flight?

Flight.

The silhouette bolted from the shadows, bursting into the moonlight that spilled across the yard and headed towards the boundary fence to Mark's left.

He took off at a sprint, ignoring the pain in his side as his old injury protested, and headed diagonally across the open space.

Too late, Aitchison's attacker realised her mistake.

Mark rugby-tackled the slight figure to the ground, then punched the soft skin and muscles on the inside of her outstretched arm.

She cried out in pain as she dropped the knife, and Mark lashed out with his foot, sweeping the weapon far away from her gloved fingers.

Aitchison's assailant struggled once more, then fell silent as bright security lights flashed to life moments before Mark heard running feet.

'Mark? Are you all right?'

Jan slid to a standstill next to him as he rolled away and clambered to his feet.

'I'm okay,' he said, keeping a firm hand on the attacker's shoulder. He reached out for the balaclava that covered the killer's features and tugged it away.

Helen Wilson glared up at him, hate in her eyes, and then turned and spat on the bare earth.

CHAPTER FORTY-SEVEN

Early the next morning, Jan finished reading out the formal caution and watched as the woman in front of her wiped her cheeks with the sleeve of her black sweatshirt.

Helen Wilson's make-up was streaked, revealing a purple bruise at her jawline that was yellowing at the outer edges. Her hair had been scraped back into a tight ponytail, accentuating her gauntness, and Jan wondered when the woman had last eaten properly.

Before last night, before the attack on Gerald Aitchison, Jan would have put the woman's countenance down to grief at the loss of Seamus Carter.

She suppressed a shudder as she recalled how Helen Wilson had fooled them all.

Next to Wilson, a duty solicitor from one of the

town's legal firms sat scribbling notes, the scratch of his fountain pen against paper a soundtrack to an otherwise silent interview room.

Finally, Turpin clasped his hands together and leaned forward, and Jan opened the manila folder in front of her that contained the documentation and photographs they intended to produce during the formal interview now underway.

'That's one hell of a bruise you've got there, Helen,' he said. 'How did you get it?'

Helen shrugged in response.

'You'll need to answer for the purposes of the recording, please.'

Turpin's voice remained calm, and Jan settled in to listen.

'I can't remember,' said Helen.

'If that's how you're going to be.' Turpin reached out and tossed the first of the photographs from the folder across the desk to where it skidded to a halt next to Helen's hands.

'Why did you kill Seamus Carter, Helen?'

The duty solicitor's brow creased at the sight of the dead priest, and then he lowered his gaze and began to write frantically in his notebook.

A darkness flittered across Helen's face, and her top lip curled. 'He deserved to die. He should have said something.'

'Said something about what?'

The woman lifted her gaze to Turpin as her fingers found the bruise on her cheek.

'My husband died because of Seamus Carter and his ilk.'

A shocked silence followed her words, and then Turpin recovered.

'You're going to have to explain that statement, Helen. You said in your initial statement to our colleagues that your husband died of a heart attack two years ago.'

A sadness swept over Wilson's face. 'Derek was under a lot of stress. He'd tried to speak to Seamus about it, but nothing happened. It broke his heart.'

'What did he speak to Seamus about?'

Helen's voice trembled. 'I didn't know at the time. Derek was never a big churchgoer but he suddenly said out of the blue that he was going to go to confession after Mass one Thursday night. We'd been talking about retaking our marriage vows, so I thought he was simply clearing the air, you know? I thought all our talk about celebrating our anniversary in style had inspired him.' She reached over to a box of tissues and plucked out two before blowing her nose. 'I knew something was wrong the moment he walked through the front door half an hour later. He seemed to have shrunk into

NONE THE WISER   333

himself – like he'd been crushed. I tried to talk to him, but—'

She broke off as sobs wracked her shoulders, and Jan eased back in her seat, a sense of dread crawling through her veins.

Turpin cleared his throat. 'What happened?'

'He died a week later,' Helen murmured. She held a fresh tissue to her eyes for a moment, then lowered her hand to her lap, her gaze falling to the photograph on the table. 'I didn't know then what had happened all those years ago. I only recently learned that.'

'How?'

'A man came to the church one Sunday afternoon, about three weeks ago. I was cleaning up after the morning service and making sure everything was in order for the evening Mass while Seamus was saying goodbye to the congregation.'

Jan pulled the artist's sketch of Simon Parkes from the folder and pushed it across the table. 'Is this the man you're referring to?'

'Yes, that's him.'

'We have a witness statement from Simon Parkes confirming he asked to speak with Seamus in private. He never mentioned you.'

'He didn't notice me, did he? Even if I am the church sacristan.' Her lips thinned. 'He looked embarrassed, furtive, as if he wasn't sure whether he should be there or not, so I decided to listen in. When I heard what he had to say, I was shocked. I decided to wait while he finished speaking with Seamus, and then I followed him out of the church when he left. I caught up with him down the lane where he'd parked his car, and said I couldn't help overhearing that he said he'd travelled from Bristol. I said that's where my husband was from.'

'Your husband, Derek, lived in Bristol?' said Mark.

'Nearby. We moved here twelve years ago.'

'What did Parkes say?'

'He told me about Hennessy – the priest who's going to be released from prison. He said Seamus was one of the few people who could make a difference. He told me he'd been abused and that he'd tried to get help, but Seamus and two other priests wouldn't listen – or chose to ignore the information.' Helen paled. 'I had no idea. I honestly had no idea. If I had, I could've saved Derek, perhaps. But I didn't know. I didn't know. Derek always told me he wanted us to move here because it was easier to get into London, but I always wondered if he tracked down Seamus and decided to keep an eye on him and the rest of them, especially after what happened.'

'Hang on. Back up,' said Mark. '*What* happened?'

'I didn't know when I first married Derek – he only told me a few days before he died. He used to act as stand-in for the organ player for a choir in a parish near Bristol.'

'Did he speak to Seamus then?' said Jan, her interest piqued.

'I don't think so – he must've been too afraid back then. I don't know why he decided to confront him when he did two years ago – maybe he thought he could atone for his silence by making things right.' Helen shrugged. 'I don't know. It doesn't matter, does it? Seamus didn't do anything at the time.'

'What else did Simon Parkes tell you?' said Mark.

'Nothing. He got embarrassed. I think he was just glad to have someone to talk to, to be honest. He gave me his phone number and asked me to get Seamus to call him if he changed his mind. He told me there were two more priests in the area who he hoped to speak to, and that if they helped then Hennessy wouldn't be released from prison. I asked him to write down their names for me so I wouldn't forget when I spoke to Seamus. I watched him walk away, get back into his car, and I knew damn well Seamus wouldn't help him. He'd never break the sacrament. He'd never tell anyone what Simon Parkes or my Derek told him during confession, and he'd never put his own position at risk to speak out against his Church.'

'And so, you killed him.'

'Yes.'

The duty solicitor's eyebrows shot upwards and he put out a restraining hand on Helen's arm, but she shook it off.

'He deserved it. They all deserved it.'

'Helen, were Philip Baxter and Robert Argyle the other names on the list?'

'Yes.'

'Did you kill Father Baxter?'

'Yes.'

Jan heard Mark take a deep breath, and then he turned to another page in the folder.

'Did you plant one of Dean Harper's plectrums at the scene of Philip Baxter's murder?'

'Yes.'

'Why?'

'Because I knew from Dean's biography on the band's website that he'd grown up near Bristol. Derek used to love that band.'

'How did you obtain the plectrum? Do you know Dean?' said Jan.

Helen smiled. 'I told you – no-one notices me. I'll bet even Terry Benedict forgot to mention I'm the one who cleans the pub every morning, didn't he?'

Mark bit back the curse that formed. 'So, you cleaned the pub on the Saturday morning and pocketed one of Dean's plectrums, then went to the church where you'd killed Seamus the night before, and raised the alarm?'

'Yes.' She looked to Jan and then back. 'Well, I still need to do my chores, don't I? If I hadn't turned up on time to clean the pub, Terry would've noticed something. Finding Dean's plectrums was luck – I knew they'd come in handy, though, so I kept one.'

Mark leaned back in his seat, his mind somersaulting over Helen's words. He pulled a photograph from Jan's file and flipped it across the table where it skidded to a halt next to Helen's elbow.

'You told us you didn't like to drive far, that you were a nervous driver,' he said. 'Those tyre marks were found on the grass verge outside Philip Baxter's house. I'm guessing they'll match your car.'

Helen's lip curled. 'I never was any good at reversing.'

'Did you intend to drop the plectrum on purpose?'

'Of course – like I said, that's why I took it.'

'Did you know Dean attended the same choir your husband had all those years ago?'

'Not to start off with, no, but when I read the biography on his website that said he was a choirboy in the same parish I figured it was too much of a coincidence.' She snorted. 'Confused you for a while, didn't it?'

Mark gestured to the engagement ring that Helen twisted on her finger as she spoke. 'Your ring – you must've known it would leave a mark on their skin, and yet you didn't take it off. Why go to all the trouble of wearing gloves to mask your fingerprints and then do that?'

A cold smile twisted the woman's face. 'I knew I had to disguise my fingerprints, but all I had were the catering gloves I use when I'm baking.'

She peered down at her ring, turning her hand as she admired the sapphire stone set within a cluster of small diamonds. 'I forgot to take this off the first time, but then when I saw the mark on Seamus's face, I thought it was so apt. I branded them, you see. Left my mark on them, just as they left their mark on Derek and the others.'

'Where are the body parts you took?' said Jan.

The woman's focus snapped back to the detective constable. 'In the chest freezer, in the garage at home. Where else would I put them?'

'What were you planning on doing with them?'

Helen pushed the photographs and sketch out of the way and leaned her arms on the table, her eyes shining.

'I was waiting until I had the whole set. Then I was going to post them to the diocesan office with a personal message for the bishop.'

Mark blinked, then checked his notes. 'Why did you attack Gerald Aitchison, Helen?'

The woman gave a derisive snort. 'He's as guilty as them. Head choirboy when my Derek was there, did you know that? Didn't speak out then, and wouldn't speak out now – especially as it'd cast a shadow over his election campaign.'

'And he and your husband never spoke about what happened all those years ago?' said Mark.

'Of course not. Both tried to put the past behind them. When Simon Parkes spoke to me and told me what was going on with that priest getting out of prison early, I knew I had to do something. Gerald wouldn't have any of it. Told me to let justice take its course.' She turned and spat on the floor. 'That's not justice.'

'Why remove Seamus's tongue and Philip's eyes?' said Mark. 'What was the point?'

'They had a chance to do something about it, and they didn't,' said Helen, wiping at her eyes. 'They pretended to see no evil, they chose never to speak out about what happened all those years ago, or hear a bad word against their Church. They chose to do nothing. They chose their God over my husband. They all did.'

CHAPTER FORTY-EIGHT

A warm current swept off the Downs and across the Vale of the White Horse the next morning when Jan climbed from the pool car and peered up at Robert Argyle's house.

Children's play equipment lay scattered across the patchy lawn of the neighbouring property, a striking contrast to the order and tidiness of Argyle's front garden. She wondered if the family would stay, or would be frightened off by the events of the past weeks.

Turpin joined her, then jerked his head towards the house.

She followed him up the path, a sense of relief tempered by exhaustion following Helen Wilson's arrest and interview. She tried not to envisage the paperwork that would be required before the case could be handed over to the Crown Prosecution Service.

'Ready?'

'Do it.'

She faced the shiny wooden surface of the replacement front door, then reached up to ring the doorbell and rapped her knuckles against the ornate glass at the top.

Moments passed, and then the sound of bolts being shot back reached Jan's ears, and she took a step back as the door opened and Robert Argyle peered over a brass security chain.

'May we come in?' she said.

'What do you want?'

'We've arrested someone in relation to your attack, and we'd like to take a statement from you,' said Turpin. He placed his hand on the door. 'So, could you let us in?'

The priest muttered under his breath as he released the chain and stood to one side while Jan led the way over the threshold.

'Come through to the kitchen,' said Argyle, shutting the door and sliding the bolts across the frame. 'I don't use the living room anymore.'

He brushed past Jan, then headed down the short narrow hallway towards the back of the house and gestured to a plain pine circular table and two chairs. 'Have a seat.'

Jan placed her bag on the floor next to her, noting the priest seemed keen to get them out of his house as soon as possible. She flipped open her notebook and recited the formal caution.

'Everything all right, Robert? You were discharged from hospital this morning, weren't you?' said Turpin.

'Yes,' said the priest. He leaned against the sink and folded his arms over his chest. 'The policeman that was outside my hospital room came in with the ward sister and said it was safe for me to come home. You said you've arrested someone?'

'Helen Wilson,' said Mark.

Jan heard the air leave the priest's lungs as he ran a hand over his mouth, his features turning grey.

'A woman?' He blinked, then turned searching eyes to them. 'But I don't know her. Why?'

'Do you recall a man by the name of Derek Wilson?' said Turpin. 'Used to play organ for the choir at the church near Bristol you belonged to.'

Argyle's Adam's apple bobbed, and he shook his head. 'I don't remember him.'

'He remembered you,' said Turpin, his voice dangerously low. 'And he told his wife, Helen. Who then systematically tortured and murdered two of your colleagues before attacking you, and then tried to kill

Gerald Aitchison. Remember him? Used to be head choir boy.'

Argyle staggered, and then reached out for the edge of the worktop and closed his eyes.

'Do you have anyone checking in on you?' said Jan.

'No. No need. I can speak to my neighbours if I need anything. I need to get back to my church. There are people who need me.'

'Tell us about George Hennessy,' said Turpin.

'There's nothing to talk about.' Argyle rounded on him, his eyes blazing. 'He was found guilty and sentenced. I had nothing to do with him, or what he was accused of.'

'You need to speak out,' said Turpin. 'Tell the authorities about the other kids. Keep him locked away, Robert. Please.'

'I can't.'

'Why not?' said Jan.

'Because it was never officially reported to me.'

'Those boys *spoke* to you in confidence,' said Turpin, his voice shaking. 'They were terrified, and they trusted you.'

'I only ever heard rumours while taking their confession,' said Argyle. 'And those matters are between them, myself and God.'

'I could take you in for formal questioning,' said

Turpin, and clenched his fists. 'You're withholding vital information to an ongoing investigation.'

Jan held up her hand. He was pushing his luck, and she needed to rein him in.

Turpin sat back in his seat, and Argyle sighed.

'It doesn't matter what you do to me in this life. This is between me and my God, and my Church. I will not – I cannot – break the sacrament. I will not divulge what is spoken to me during the process of reconciliation.'

'Robert, I need your help,' said Turpin and leaned forward, his eyes beseeching. 'I can't understand why you won't help my colleagues pursue their investigation into the systematic abuse that is alleged to have occurred.'

'I don't expect you to understand,' snapped Argyle. 'That's my point.'

'Can you imagine what those children went through? The damage that's been done?'

'No, and nor would I want to. But let me ask you this, Detective Turpin. Can you imagine what it would be like to be ex-communicated from your Church? To be ostracised by the only community you ever knew? To be cast aside by your religion, by your God?'

Argyle broke off, shaking his head.

'Look, we'll need a formal statement from you in relation to what you can tell us about Helen Wilson,' said Jan, her voice calm as her eyes bored into the priest's. 'She will be charged for assaulting you, and for the murders of Seamus Carter and Philip Baxter. But, DS Turpin is right – it doesn't end there. It can't end there. These are serious allegations being made against Father Hennessy.'

'And that's all they are. Allegations. No proof,' said Argyle. He pursed his lips. 'That's all I have to say on the matter.'

Turpin slammed his palm on the table and rose from his chair. He looked down at the priest, and waited until the man's eyes locked with his.

'I hope to hell your excuses pass muster with your God when you meet Him,' he said.

CHAPTER FORTY-NINE

Mark tapped the razor on the side of the ceramic washbasin, then flushed it through the soapy water before pulling out the plug.

Steam from the shower clouded towards the open circular window that faced the river, sunlight dappling his shoulders as he towelled himself dry.

He whistled in tune to the radio in the galley, a familiar eighties rock anthem buoying his mood.

DI Kennedy had awarded the investigation team an early finish before heading to a media conference to announce the arrest of the "priest butcher", as the local rag had so eloquently labelled her.

Jan had wandered over to him as they were packing up their desks for the afternoon. 'Do you want to come over to ours for a barbecue tonight? Mum's got the boys for the weekend so we can relax and have a few beers. Scott can buy some steaks and whatnot on the way home.'

Mark's stomach rumbled at the memory, and he pushed his way through the narrow doorway that led to the bedroom.

After tearing a comb through his unruly hair, he pulled on jeans and a polo shirt before walking through the cabin, checking the windows were closed.

Satisfied the narrowboat was secure enough that Lucy and his other neighbours would spot any intruders, he flicked off the radio and shrugged a leather jacket over his shoulders.

He checked his hair in the mirror next to the back hatch of the narrowboat, then slipped Hamish's lead off the hook and stepped outside.

'Ooh, look at you.'

He peered across the deck to see Lucy standing on the towpath, her arms crossed and a cheeky grin teasing her lips.

'Hot date?' she said.

Mark felt his face grow warm, and bent down to clip the lead to Hamish's collar. 'Dinner with a colleague and her husband.'

'Good. No need for me to be jealous, then.'

She grinned, then threw a wave over her shoulder

and continued along the towpath to a neighbouring cabin cruiser.

Mark watched her for a moment, then realising two other walkers were staring at him with bemused expressions, cleared his throat and climbed from the gunwale.

'Come on,' he said to Hamish.

The towpath into town was busy with late afternoon dog walkers, joggers and couples with pushchairs.

The summer boat hire season was starting in earnest and he raised his hand in greeting to the passengers on two cruisers that passed him, the shouts and excited banter from those on board carrying across the water.

He only hoped they didn't moor next to him on their return, spoiling the peace and quiet he relished.

When he reached the main road, he turned right, crossed the bridge into town and set a quick pace through the centre towards Peachcroft.

Hamish trotted along at his heels, happy to explore, his nose in the air and his tail wagging.

Mark pulled out his phone to check Jan's address on the maps app, and turned into the cul-de-sac.

He slowed as he drew level with number sixteen, his confusion turning to horror.

Through the double-glazed panes of an upstairs

bedroom window came the unmistakable sound of two trombones duelling for noise domination.

'Oh, God.'

Hamish whined, turned tail and pulled on his lead.

'No, you don't. If I'm going to be subjected to this, then so are you.'

The dog's brown eyes stared up at him dolefully.

'It's a barbecue. There are probably sausages.'

Hamish wagged his tail, but his eyes remained uncertain.

'You can have two.'

Mark took a deep breath, then reached out for the doorbell.

Before he could press it, the door opened and Jan slipped through the gap, her bag slung over one shoulder and a jacket over her arm.

She held up a hand and put a finger to her lips.

'What's going on, Jan? Barbecue cancelled or something?'

'My mother phoned half an hour ago – she was meant to be having the boys to stay this weekend, but something's come up.'

'Do you want to do this another night, then?'

'Hell, no.' She put her hand on his arm and steered him along the garden path and through the gate. 'I'm not staying in there a moment longer – it's bedlam.'

'So where are we going?'

'The pub. I'm buying dinner.'

THE END

ABOUT THE AUTHOR

Before turning to writing, *USA Today* bestselling author Rachel Amphlett played guitar in bands, dabbled in radio as a presenter and freelance producer for the BBC, and worked in publishing as an editorial assistant.

She now wields a pen instead of a plectrum and writes crime fiction and spy thrillers, including the fast paced *Dan Taylor* and *English Assassins* espionage novels, and the *Detective Kay Hunter* British murder mystery series.

After 13 years in Australia, Rachel has returned to the UK and is now based in the picturesque county of Dorset.

You can find out more about her writing at www. rachelamphlett.com.